BULLETTIME

By E. Faison

Mesa, Arizona USA

ISBN 978-0-6151-6637-7

Buy this book or download it at:

www.lulu.com

Printed in the United States of America.

Acknowledgements

I'd like to acknowledge everyone who supported me in creating this book. It was your feedback and encouragement that got me to go through with it. So thank you to the following people: my parents, Tiffany, Elijah, Samuel, Nikki, and Demetrios. Also, I'd like to acknowledge Rockstar Games, Remedy, Take Two, Warner Bros, Andy Wachowski, and Larry Wachowski. Lastly, the following entities are in my book because they have inspired me in one way or another: John Woo, Chow Yun Fat, Glock, Heckler & Koch, Taurus, SigArms, Benelli, Beretta, Ruger, Desert Eagle, Colt, Barrett, Mossberg, DC Comics, RedBull, Rockstar, Armani, Prada, Fendi, Versace, Affliction, True Religion, Christian Dior, Sony, Apple, Hennessey, Grey Goose, Absolut, Stoli, Courvoisier, Heineken, White Castle, Audi, Mazda, Ford, General Motors, West Coast Choppers, Harley Davidson, Killswitch Engage, Mobb Deep, Atreyu, Aiden, Him, AFI, Motorhead, Prince, Kid & Ruben, Eva Longoria, Chuck Norris, the cities of Detroit, Gulfport, New Orleans, Bay St. Louis, New York, Phoenix, Miami, and Windsor. Thanks and apologies to anyone I forgot. Richard, Jarrod, Chris! Peace!

E. FAISON

"If, upon my death, I am to be judged for all of my sins…I only hope to have a really good defense attorney"- Ash Calibre

E. FAISON

Contents

BULLETTIME

<u>Chance In Hell</u>

BULLETTIME

Midnight. The Mississippi fog was so thick I could slice it with my combat knife. We were in a black Mazda CX9, outside of Club Darqcyde. The club, located in Gulfport, was owned by an infamous group from Mississippi. The Wraiths. Some called them a biker gang, some called them a militia. They liked to refer to themselves as an organization. Either way, they were dangerous. They were responsible for 13 homicides in the past six months, and were the sole controllers of the Gulfs meth industry. They also owned and ran Iron Cross Casino, nearby in Bay St. Louis.

More than just a business front, this was their prime source of income. Last year alone, they raked in an estimated $2.4 million in legitimate gambling. And that's aside from their various illegal activities which included money laundering, prostitution, blackmail, larceny, and god knows what else.

They seemed able to avoid too much attention from the feds, partially because they had plenty of political figures in their pockets. And the fact that they record everything that goes on at Iron Cross didn't hurt either. Vacationing politicians always seemed to stop by the casino's hotel for a little Hedonistic activity.

The Wraiths seemed to be nearly untouchable. And I did my research well. But then again, I never attempted to capture a fugitive without learning as much as possible about said fugitive, and his associates.

I'd been in the business for too long to make the mistake of underestimating anyone. But I'd promised my wife this was my final job. And as I sat, deep in thought, outside of that club, I wished my job before this was my final job. I had been a bounty hunter for twenty-seven years, and I was good at it. One of the best. But I was also tired.

I'd earned enough money to live comfortably for the rest of my life. But I had a hard time walking away from the career I love. I guess it's the thrill of the hunt. But it was time to cash in my chips. I was approaching fifty, and retirement in Phoenix was calling.

Unfortunately though, that retirement would be short lived. I was given about a year to live, due to Cirrhosis of the liver. The many years of alcohol abuse had finally caught up with me. And donor livers usually went to people who were suffering from cancer, or liver disease, or some sort of terminal ailment that wasn't caused by alcohol or drugs. Those were the ones who deserved transplants. Once in a while, an old drunk like me would get lucky, but not often.

But I'd beaten the odds before. I'd

cheated death on several occasions, and maybe, just maybe I could prove my doctor wrong. But my life insurance policy didn't cover death by cognac. So the money that I had saved throughout my career was for my wife Marie. For when I'm gone. Damn Hennessy. That was my nectar, my poison. Hennessy. Dark and smooth, but with a kick. Just like myself.

"Yo EZ, you ready to do this or what?" a grimy southern voice interrupted my thoughts. It was 23 year old Jarrod O'Connor in the passenger seat. He was my back up for this particular job. I usually worked alone, but considering the people we were dealing with, I decided to take on a partner. Plus he knew the area well. O'Connor was a 6'5" 285lb beast from New Orleans. He participated in a few cage fighting tournaments, and was in the process of making quite a name for himself, before cracking a vertebrae in a motorcycle accident.

After recovering from the near-paralyzing experience, Jarrod decided to focus on his "day job", Bail Enforcement. He felt that there was less of a chance of re-injuring his back that way. Go figure. "Yeah. Its time," I replied, "but remember... be assertive, yet non-confrontational. I notified GPD of the situation, but it doesn't look like they'll be making an appearance." Not that I expected or wanted their help. Cops don't have as much jurisdiction as bounty hunters, and they could sometimes prove to be more of a hindrance than assistance. But it never hurt to have them present, in case things turn ugly.

"Yeah, well fuck 'em! Most of 'em are on the Wraiths' payroll anyway." Jarrod retorted. I proceeded to do a quick weapons check: Desert Eagle .50 caliber in my shoulder holster; Taurus Millennium .40 caliber on my right hip; Glock 9mm on my left hip; combat knife in my left boot; and handcuffs in my back pocket. I looked over at Jarrod. He was armed with twin Ruger .45s and a shit-eating grin.

We stepped out of the SUV simultaneously, almost synchronized. I inhaled the thick fog like second hand smoke and slid my leather trenchcoat on over my bullet-proof vest. "That's so cliché," Jarrod snickered. "Bounty hunter with a fuckin' trenchcoat." I glance at Jarrod: big White guy wearing a cowboy hat, jean jacket, blue Levis and cowboy boots. Then I looked at myself: Black and bald, 5'9, 180lbs, wearing a knee length trenchcoat, black jeans and black boots. "Yeah, well we both kinda look like low budget action movie rejects." I smiled.

As we made our way through the dimly lit parking lot, I took another look at the fugitive's Polaroid from the bonds office. White male, 6'2", 255, long brown hair, and a thin goatee. Cyril Gallant.

He skipped out on a $300,000 bond. The charge: 1st degree murder. The bonds-man, Demetrios Sims, got word that Gallant was hiding out at the club, possibly living in a back room or something. The problem was that the doors stayed locked until the club opens, which was right around midnight. And supposedly Gallant never left the club. But the information came from a solid source.

That's when Sims called me. I usually worked in the Motor City, but I'd work anywhere in America, Canada or Mexico for the right fee. Sims knew my services weren't cheap. 20% of the bond, plus all expenses. But he also knew my level of skill. I'd done many jobs for him before. Jobs that most of my colleagues wouldn't touch for whatever reason, (either they we too stupid or just too chicken shit). But I completed the jobs, and recovered the fugitives. All of them. It isn't rocket science, its fucking bail enforcement. And Sims was counting on me one last time. So I was not about to let him down.

As O'Connor and I walked towards the big red neon sign that read "Darqcyde", and the front door underneath it, I look around the parking lot. About a dozen assorted motorcycles (mostly Harleys), a Hummer H2, and a '87 Camaro. As we got closer, I noticed a grotesquely overweight man standing by the door, posing as a bouncer. I could hear heavy metal blaring inside.

"My Last Serenade." Jarrod grinned. "What?" I snapped at him. "The song playing. It's 'My Last Serenade', by Killswitch Engage." I gave him a rotten look and grunted "How 'bout you focus on the task at hand, and not the fuckin' music?" He put his head down, like a scolded puppy.

As we got to the door, the fat man started cracking his knuckles. "Can I help you?" Jarrod and I both were wearing our badges in plain view. Mine was on a chain around my neck, hanging over my chest. Jarrod's was on his belt, next to his big ass buckle.

"My name is Ezekiel Grey, this is Jarrod O'Connor. We're bail enforcement agents and we're going inside." I was straight to the point. The man raised his left hand, "You guys can't come in he-aahh!" Before the bouncer could finish his sentence, Jarrod grabbed his hand and with one quick motion, twisted his arm and delivered a powerful right hook to his left temple. He dropped like a bag of shit. "That's what you call non confrontational?" I frowned, looking at the fallen doorman's unconscious carcass. "Nah, I call that just warming up." Jarrod smirked, rubbing his knuckles.

I felt like I had just stepped into a bad Chuck Norris flick. I wanted to apprehend Gallant with as little collateral damage as possible. And this wild cowboy was already ruining that plan. "I'm in charge here, goddamn it," I shouted, "And we're not going to use force unless I say so!" Jarrod just smirked and asked "Well, he's out of our way right?" I just shook my head and muttered "Come on."

He did have a point, but experience told me that with a gang like this, if you show force, they'll only answer back with greater force. And I knew that if we had a chance in Hell of taking down Gallant, we'd need to approach with caution, not aggression.

As I pushed open the front door, the thick fog was replaced with even thicker smoke. The funk of tobacco and marijuana was almost over-powering. There were about a dozen men and six women in the room. Not very populated, but seeing as how the

club just opened, I was sure it would get bus-
ier as time went on. And I was hoping to be
long gone by then.

The club was one level, and about
two thousand square feet, pretty cozy. It
hardly qualified as a club where I was from.
More like a dive bar. It consisted of a dance
floor, maybe ten tables, and a wall length
bar. The music was at a deafening level,
pouring out of two huge speakers hooked up
to some hi-tech juke-box.

As we strolled casually towards the
bar, I peered around the room, attempting to
identify our fugitive. One by one, the patrons stopped what they were doing and
stared at us. I made eye contact with each
person, keeping a stone glare on my face.
"What can I get for you, uhh, gentlemen?"
The middle aged barkeep looked almost as
disgusted as he did disgusting. His face was
plagued with crack-ne, his lips were badly
chapped, and he wore a raggedy toupee.

"Information," I replied. "I'm looking for this man. Heard I could find him
here." I placed the Polaroid on the bar. Now

I've always been pretty good at reading people's reactions, but the barkeep made it a little too obvious. Upon taking one look at the picture, he almost immediately revealed Gallant's location by shooting a quick glance to his left. "Never seen him." he mumbled. "Now you boys best be on your way." He seemed nervous and wasn't good at lying. I looked to the barkeep's left and notice a door with a large red and white sign on it that read 'Office, Keep Out'. I took a step towards the door.

"Don't even think about goin' back there" The barkeep's voice was shaky, "Not without a fuckin' warrant." Jarrod drew a .45 out of his right side hip holster. "This is all the warrant we need, asshole." he spat. We stepped toward the door, Jarrod on my right side, and I drew my Desert Eagle.

I've arrested thousands of bail jumpers over the years, but I got the adrenaline rush every time. This was no different. But I could always tell when something wasn't right. And this time, something just felt...very wrong.

BULLETTIME

A 12-gauge shotgun being cocked has a distinct sound. The song had ended. The club was virtually silent as the patrons looked on. And we were two feet from the office door when I heard that bone chilling sound. It came from behind us, but before I could turn around, a thunderous <BOOM> filled my eardrums, nearly shattering them.

The right side of my face was suddenly splashed with thick warm liquid and hard chunks of something I couldn't yet identify. I turn to my right just in time to see a headless Jarrod O'Connor take a final step, before collapsing to the floor, blood gushing from the crater that used to be his head, like lava from an erupting volcano. It was then that I realized the liquid that splashed my face was Jarrod's blood, and the chunks were pieces of his skull and brain. "Ooooh!" someone shouted. I heard a few screams and then silence. It happened so fast, yet for that moment, things seemed to be taking place in slow motion.

Suddenly, I heard the familiar sound again, as the barkeep chambered another round into his boom-stick of death. Still holding my Desert Eagle, I quickly spun around to face the barkeep, and fired three rounds in his direction. I didn't even aim. No time. I just pointed and squeezed. The 1st and 2nd shots hit liquor bottles behind the bar. Damn recoil. It didn't matter. With a .50 caliber hand cannon, you only need one shot. The 3rd bullet struck the barkeep just under his left eye, pushing most of his brain out the back of his head, and taking half of his face with it. As the back of his head burst open, blood splashed a row of vodka bottles.

Just then, the office door swung open behind me, and I turned back around to come face to face with... "Gallant!" I shouted and put the gun to his head.

Gallant's appearance had changed. His head was now shaved, and he had a full thick beard. But I'd studied the Polaroid and his booking mugshot for long enough. And those eyes were a dead give-away, even as they doubled in size when my gun touched his forehead.

"Turn around and put your hands on

your fucking head!" I commanded. I then heard two shots go off, and I was struck in the back twice. It felt and sounded like a .380, not too powerful. Nevertheless, I was glad I had on my vest.

With my left hand I grabbed my Glock, and keeping the Desert Eagle on Gallant, I turned and pointed the Glock toward the direction of the fired shots. It was a scrawny looking kid about 18 years old. He looked like he could use a meal and a shower. He had a hateful scowl on his face and was wearing a filthy Wraiths motorcycle jacket.

"Fuckin nigger, you 'bout ta die!" he shouted, and as he raised the pistol to fire again, time seemed to slow down. I could feel my heart beating through my chest. My adrenaline was running high, my senses seemed to elevate.

My intentions were not to take down anyone but my intended target. But it was too late for that. Now it seemed that this mission would turn into a blood bath before the night was over.

Before the kid could fire again, I

launched two hollow point 9mm slugs into his chest. His knees buckled as both rounds hit him in the heart. I heard gasping from the onlookers, who were mostly ducking for cover. As the kid fell backwards, his arms stayed stiff, and he fired another round, which hit the ceiling above him. His arms then dropped by his sides, and he laid still.

My eyes scanned the club for other would-be assailants looking to die by my hand. No one was ready to step up. I turned my head back towards Gallant, only to have it bashed with a crowbar. Gallant must've grabbed it when I wasn't looking. The impact nearly knocked me out cold as it ripped open my forehead, just above my left eyebrow. I hit the ground hard, but was back on my feet instantly. Gallant wasn't worth shit to me dead, but he was pushing it. He swung the crowbar again, this time I dodged it. The iron melee weapon hit the wall and stuck in it. I put the Desert Eagle to Gallant's right hand and detached it from the crowbar by pulling the trigger.

"Aaaaahh!" Gallant screamed, grabbing what was left of his hand, which now consisted of a thumb, an index finger, and a mangled bloody nub. He fell backwards, inside the office he called home, and I followed him in. I holstered the Glock and reached for my handcuffs. Ignoring his painful howls, I took a quick glance around the office. There wasn't much to it besides an old ratty futon, a broken dresser, a small TV and a PlayStation 2. The floor was littered with fast food bags, pizza boxes, and various articles of dirty clothing. The room smelled like a dumpster.

I noticed my reflection in a cracked mirror on the wall. My face was a crimson mess. Jarrod's drying blood and brains on the right side, my own fresh blood on the left. I resembled some neo-gladiator in the midst of the fight of his life. The vision in my left eye was slightly blurred as blood from my gaping head wound leaked into it, and continued down my face like sweat from a marathon runner. 'That's gonna need stiches,' I thought to myself.

The mirror suddenly shattered as it was struck by a bullet that was meant for me.

'Goddamn it', I thought. 'Won't they give up?'
It was the doorman. He still looked dazed and
he stumbled as he fired another round from
his .38 snub. This one struck me in the left
shoulder, less than an inch from my vest. The
pain was too familiar, and I winced as I returned fire with the Desert Eagle. One shot to
the gut, and one to the chin, shattering his jaw.
The third shot was high and wide, missing him
by a few inches. His eyes grew wide as he
dropped the gun and, with both hands,
grabbed what was left of his face. He slowly
slumped back against the wall behind him and
slid down to the floor, leaving two smudged
trails of blood on the wall.

I holstered the .50 cal, grabbed Gallant's left wrist and slapped the cuffs on it. I
twisted it back and grabbed his right arm.
"Aaaah! you mother fucker!" Gallant was in
tremendous pain. I cuffed his right wrist.
"Don't resist, and this will all be over soon." I
tried to sound confident, but I wasn't even
sure I'd make it out of there. I was starting to
feel a little dizzy, and I had to keep winking
my left eye to keep from being blinded by the

blood flowing into it.

I heard another shot, and felt a hot piercing pain in my right thigh. Before this night, I'd taken 13 bullets in my career. And each time it hurt like hell. It's a pain you just never get used to.

"Don't move" I ordered Gallant, and drew the .40 cal. I spun around to see a girl, about 17, pointing the same .380 the scrawny kid had. "You killed Tommy you cock-sucker!" Her voice sounded like a screeching eagle, swooping down on its fleeing meal. I pointed the .40 and hesitated. She was young and very pretty. Long dark hair. Large doe-like eyes. Tears running her mascara down her angry, frightened face. She somewhat reminded me of my daughter Eliza.

"Don't fuckin' do it man, she's just a kid!" I glanced to my left and spotted a man with a handle-bar mustache and no shirt on. He looked about 40 and was covered with tattoos from his neck down. He had just picked up one of Jarrod's .45s, and was rais-ing it in my direction. The girl fired another round, and time slowed down. I saw the

26

muzzle flash, and felt like I could see the bullet approach me, but I froze.

The bullet struck my right cheek, grazing the bone, and continuing to my ear. "Uuunnhh!" I cried out in disbelief, and grabbed my face with my left hand, .40 caliber still pointed at the girl. The upper half of my right ear was gone, and I could feel the canyon in my cheek gushing blood. "Bitch!" I shouted as I drew the Glock with my left hand, and as she fired another shot, I dove backwards.

Time once again seemed to slow down, this time to a near halt. In mid air, I brought my legs up until my body was level, completely horizontal. I opened fire with both pistols, shooting the girl with the .40 cal and the tattoo man with the 9mm. I caught the girl in her liver, her left breast, and the right side of her forehead. The man was struck in the groin, the ribs, and the center of his chest. The subsequent shots missed, but I emptied both clips before I hit the floor. I landed flat on my back and felt like resting there for a while. I was in a lot of pain. But I thought to myself, 'Can't rest yet, got to take care of business.'

I dropped the Glock, and popped in another clip to the .40 caliber. I quickly stood up. "Anyone else feeling suicidal?" I roared, "Fuck with me!!" Though the remaining people openly objected to what was taking place, they didn't seem like they wanted to chance losing their lives as well. They were crouched down in a group like hostages, hands raised. I wanted them to know that I was prepared to kill every motherfucker in the club if I had to. But I had to move fast. I was losing a lot of blood, and I wouldn't be able to take much more damage in that condition.

"I need a fuckin' doctor" Gallant moaned. I looked over at him. His hand was bleeding uncontrollably, soaking the back of his pants completely. He was hunched over, hands firmly cuffed behind his back. But I felt no pity whatsoever. "Then tell your people to back the fuck down!" I barked at him. "Ay, everybody, chill the fuck out! I'm dyin'

over here!" He sounded sincere, but I wasn't
sure if they'd listen.

I picked up the Glock, holstered it,
and pulled Gallant up by the back of his
shirt. "Let's go!" I ordered, and he obliged. I
slowly walked behind him to the door, and in
a constant sweeping motion, I pointed the
.40 at each person in the club. The remaining
patrons looked terrified, but I didn't care.
"No one fuckin' move" I yelled. And no one
did.

We reached the door and quickened
the pace. "Double-time! Move!" I shouted.
"Where to?" Gallant sounded bewildered.
"Black Mazda SUV!" I would have broken
into a full sprint if my thigh didn't hurt so
much from the bullet in it.

We were halfway to the vehicle,
when a man on a custom chopper pulled
into the lot. He took one look at me, and
killed the engine. "What the fuck is going
on?" he demanded. Not wanting to deal with
any more bullshit, I just fired four shots into
his torso, sending his lifeless body flying off
the chopper, and into the row of other mo-

torcycles. That created a domino effect, as each motorcycle fell over, one by one.

We reached the vehicle and I didn't hesitate. I opened the passenger side and pushed Gallant in, slamming the door behind him. I ran to the driver side, and jumped in behind the wheel. I started the ignition, and peeled out.

"Can you see in this fog, man?" Gallant was starting to panic. I didn't respond. I could barely see five feet in front of the SUV, and switching the headlights to bright only made it worse. I wasn't used to driving in fog this thick. It never got this bad in Motown. But I was determined to get as far away from Darqcyde as possible. I needed to make it to a hospital. The worst part was over, I survived another shootout. And although my face had been disfigured, I was happy to be alive. I knew Marie would be happy to see me, regardless of my new look. But I also knew a great plastic surgeon out in Phoenix, just in case.

I was hauling ass, doing about 95mph. The road was winding and there were a few other cars out. I came to a red light and screeched to a halt. I was a couple of miles from the club, so I started to relax a little. But I was lost. "Where's the nearest hospital?" I asked Gallant. He was leaned over against the door. "T-two m-m-miles...up. Broad Avenue. M-make a right." He didn't sound too good.

"Aw, c'mon you pussy! It's only a flesh wound. Look at my *face*, for Christ's sake!" I tried to make light of the situation, but in reality I knew that if I didn't find an emergency room quick, we'd both be fucked. 'Goddamn red light,' I thought. 'I'm just gonna run it'.

That's when I saw the headlights in the rearview mirror. Only for a couple of seconds, but for those two seconds, I couldn't react fast enough. It was a Hummer, and it was barreling at us like some raging bull, charging a Matador.

I remembered the Hummer in the club parking lot, and I stomped on the accelerator. But I was too late. As the tires spun out on the moist road, the Hummer rear-

31

ended us with the force of a mighty tsunami. There was an ear-shattering explosion of metal and glass, and then…blackness.

"Sir? Sir, can you hear me?" I woke up on my back, in a puddle of my own blood, about 20 feet from the twisted wreckage. The CX9 was in flames and I could smell the burning flesh inside. Gallant was being barbecued alive, and he let out one long, blood-curdling scream. Then he was silent.

There was a man wearing a torn Italian suit kneeling next to me. He was staring at the burning vehicle. "Fuck, I didn't know there was someone else in there," he muttered, and looked down at me. "I called 911, the paramedics are on the way, stay with me sir!" The concerned, slightly slurred voice belonged to an awful smelling fellow, about my age. He reeked of liquor and weed. He was also bleeding from the head, and looked frazzled.

"I'm so sorry about this. But I'll take care of everything. Don't worry about a thing. Just hang on!" I recognized the man.

He was Tony Brigade, former mayor of Biloxi. He had planned to run for President in
the last election, but bowed out after some
guy claimed to have a sex tape starring Brigade and two prostitutes. The man went
missing shortly after that, and the tape never
surfaced. Brigade resigned following the incident, an almost certain admission of guilt. I
guess part of me should have been relieved
that it was him, and not the Hummer from
the club.

"Hang on, they're coming now,"
Brigade announced cheerfully. I tried to ask
what happened, but I couldn't speak. I just
let out a gurgling noise. My jaw was broken,
and I felt an unbearable pressure on my
chest. 'Collapsed lungs', I thought to myself.
I couldn't move. I started to panic, but tried
to control it. "Stay with me, goddamn it,
Hang on!" Brigade pled, but I could feel myself slipping away.

He started to pace back and forth.
"I'm sorry...I'm so sorry. I got completely
wasted at Glory Holes, and lost track of time.
I was trying to hurry home to my wife. I did-

n't even see your SUV until the last moment."

'No fucking way!' I thought to myself. Glory Holes was a seedy strip bar, just up the road from Darqcyde. I'd been there about a year earlier, to arrest the owner for a Failure to appear warrant. The bar was a real cesspool of drunken debauchery. It employed bottom-of-the-barrel strippers, willing to suck for a buck, and was a favorite to the city's lowlifes and hoodlums. I had no idea what the former mayor was doing at that place, but I couldn't worry about that. I was dying. And I couldn't believe what I was hearing. To survive what I just went through, what I'd been going through for 27 years, only to be done in by a drunken mayor out for a fucking lap-dance?!

This was an outrage! I tried to stand up. I needed to kick the shit out of Brigade. But I couldn't move a muscle. Panic once again set in, but this time I couldn't control it. I felt helpless. Every bone in my body was probably broken.

I could hear the sirens, screaming in

the distance. But they wouldn't make it in time. The puddle of blood was rapidly growing, and started to look more like a pond. I could feel darkness consuming me, like a starving maggot consuming rotten flesh.

I wished I could see Marie one more time. I needed to tell her how much I loved her, how sorry I was for all the mistakes I'd ever made. And my only daughter, Eliza. What I would've given to see her beautiful face again. She was expecting her first child the following month. A little boy, to be named Elijah. I was supposed to be a grandfather. But I'll never know my grandson.

Well, at least I beat the cirrhosis. I didn't want to die that way anyway. I'd much rather die doing what I loved. And if this was as close as I could get to doing that, then well…I'll take it. So tired…

They say that before you die, your life flashes before your eyes. That didn't happen for me. No white light at the end of a tunnel. No angel to greet me at the Pearly Gates. Not even a Grim Reaper. Just darkness. And silence. And… PEACE.

BULLETTIME

Prologue:

I have this recurring nightmare that I'm drowning in a swimming pool. I hit the bottom of the pool, feet first, and I try my damnedest to jump up to the surface and yell for help. I make it up a couple of times, but only for a second. And then I'm back underwater, fighting for my life. What's odd is, the whole time this is happening, I'm still breathing. But I'm breathing water, not air. The whole ordeal lasts maybe ten minutes, until suddenly I wake up, drenched in sweat and gasping for breath.

This dream occurs about twice a month, and this was one of those nights.

I never could figure out why I'd get the dream. I never learned to swim. Hell, I never had a reason. I grew up in the Queensbridge housing projects in New York. There were no swimming pools, just pools of blood. Murder was an everyday thing in Queens. As a youth I'd seen more dead people than the kid from that M. Night movie. Only the ones I saw didn't talk. They just laid there and stunk. The sight and smell of rotting corpses warped my mind at an early age.

And as if I wasn't screwed up enough, I never knew my dad. He was in prison when I was born, and for all I knew, he was still there. Yeah, yeah…poor, fatherless kid growing up in the projects. Heard the story before right? Wrong. I was the product of rape. My mother was 16 at the time, living in New Orleans, Louisiana with her parents. She was walking home from cheer practice one evening when some bastard grabbed her and forced her into his van. Apparently he had been stalking her for weeks, leaving notes and flowers at her front door. She thought nothing of it, assuming it was a guy at her school, not some 30yr old predator.

It was a different time, the early eighties. Parents were less cautious. But back then, there were less psychotic pedophiles running wild. But he was captured a few weeks after the assault, thanks to the fingerprints he left on the various gifts he'd leave at the doorstep. At his trial he had the nerve to say he was in love with her, and that he planned to marry her. Fucking loony tunes. His demented testimony fell upon deaf ears, and the judge threw the book at him. But the celebration was short lived, as a follow up doctor's visit revealed my existence.

When my mother found out she was pregnant, her southern Baptist parents suddenly changed their Pro-life stance. They tried to talk their daughter into getting an abortion. Personally, I think it was partially due to the fact that the man that raped her was White. But she felt that there was no way she could end an innocent life, regardless of the circumstances. So she caught hell from basically her whole family, for going through with the pregnancy.

When she turned 18, determined that she and I could make it on our own, she packed up, and moved us to Queens. She wanted to get as far away from her family as possible. My mother was a strong Black woman from New Orleans, but New York was a whole different world. And the older I got, the more I resembled my father. Every time my mom saw me, she saw a spitting image of her assailant.

When I was 15, she started using heroine. I couldn't be mad at her, I was the one selling it to her. I was too coked up half the time to care about anything or anyone.

Growing up I was one of a few racially mixed kids in my neighborhood, and at first I got picked on. A lot. Numerous suspensions from different schools, and several arrests were all due to fighting. But that's how I learned to stand up for myself, and eventually, I was accepted by the other kids.

The funny thing is that I wanted to be a cop when I grew up. Not that I wanted to clean up the mean streets or any bullshit like that. I just watched a lot of cop shows as a kid, and I thought it'd be cool to shoot bad guys. But things change.

When I was 16, I did a couple of years in juvie for pistol whipping one of my customers. I beat the poor bastard within an inch of his life. While I was locked up, my mom took a crack and heroine cocktail and overdosed. The neighbors called the police a week later when the smell became unbearable. I didn't go to the funeral.

I was released a week before my 18th birthday, and just two months after 9/11. On my own for the first time, I was determined to get my shit together… well sort of. My record as an adult was clean. But I was no longer interested in being an officer of the law. I decided to pursue another career. A better career, with lower standards, and a higher pay scale. My name is Ash Calibre and I'm an assassin for hire.

BULLETTIME

E. FAISON

<u>HellBent</u>

BULLETTIME

After waking from the familiar night-

mare, I opened my eyes to an empty fifth of

Grey Goose vodka, a bunch of empty Heine-

ken bottles, traces of cocaine on a compact

mirror, and a naked Dominican woman. She

appeared to be sleeping, so I was glad to see she

was alive. You never know, right?

What the fuck happened last night? I

got out of the semen-stained bed and stretched.

My head felt like it had been tap-danced on by

Mr. Bojangles for about eight hours. I ran my

hand through my straight, black, shoulder length hair and looked down at the compact mirror. As I started lining up what was left of the coke, I noticed my gray eyes were blood-shot. "Fuck," I mumbled. The woman suddenly woke up. "Hey, sexy. You ready to go another round?" She purred. She resembled a younger, dirtier version of Eva Longoria. She had long, brown hair that was a complete mess. I noticed bite marks on her breasts that matched my teeth, and bruises on her neck, thighs, and above her vagina. This one liked it rough. And apparently I accommodated her.

She rolled over on her stomach, and I licked my lips. "Great ass!" I smiled. She rolled her eyes, "I know. You kept telling me that last night, when your tongue was in it." I winked at her and put on my briefs. I noticed a half bottle of Heineken and the question of 'is the bottle half empty or half full?' came to mind. 'Fuck it. It's empty now', I thought, as I chugged the warm liquid. Anything to get that shitty taste out of my mouth.

I was in a low rate hotel in Windsor, Ontario, Canada. It was all coming back to me as I strolled out to the balcony. The job. The woman in the room wanted to pay me $20,000 to kill her husband, James Tucker. He was the 52 year old President of a used car dealership in Detroit called Motor City Motors. Catchy name, I know, but they were actually one of the more successful small dealerships in the city.

Wealthy and naive, he married a girl he'd only dream of getting if he wasn't well off. He wasn't quite rich, but he did have a multi-million dollar life insurance policy. And his 19 year-old Latina vixen Melissa stood to gain a lot from his demise. But Tucker was smarter than she thought. And he was a few steps ahead of her. Tucker actually hired me about two weeks prior to keep an eye on her.

You see, I'm not really an assassin. I'm a Private Investigator. So I lied in the prologue. Bite me, the rest was 100% true.

Tucker suspected Melissa was cheating on him, and wanted proof. He was referred to me by a mutual friend in Detroit. He wanted me to follow Melissa around, get video and audio recordings, even proposition her if need be. He just wanted proof of infidelity. And he was paying me $200 a day plus expenses to get that proof.

After two weeks of tailing Melissa to the spa, the gym, the salon, and other typical upper middle class housewife places of leisure, I was getting no dirt on her. Tucker was ready to pull the plug. I convinced him to let me try a more direct approach, and he agreed. So I approached her that night. During the two weeks of tailing her, I had built up quite an attraction to her, but I knew crossing the line was bad business.

But I also had a reputation as a P.I. to uphold. And if she was cheating, I was determined to find out. What I did know is that she and Tucker argued constantly. I had numerous hours of their disputes on tape. Mostly petty bullshit. They just were two very different people. It was obvious Tucker married her for her looks, and she married him for his money, but you'd think they'd at least *try* to get along.

Approaching Melissa was easy. I ran into her outside of her Yoga class. Literally. I backed into her Range Rover. Just tapped the bumper, but enough to get her attention. After giving me a verbal thrashing, she calmed down enough for me to use my charm on her. I've always had a way with women. And my looks didn't hurt either. I've been told I resembled a masculine version of Prince in his prime.

It didn't take long before Melissa agreed to join me for dinner. She followed me to Windsor, and we wined and dined at a little French restaurant. I got into her head, and she fell in lust. By the end of the evening, she was begging to run away with me. Tucker wanted his proof, right? We got the hotel, and I produced plenty of verification that Melissa was unfaithful. The questions was; was she cheating on him before I came along? Or did Tucker just sponsor it by hiring me? Oh well. I couldn't care less. I had a blast.

That's when she dropped the bomb on me. She wanted Tucker dead, and she wanted his money. She had been planning to end him for months, but she just didn't know anyone who'd do it. I entertained her plot by agreeing to slash Tucker's throat, which turned the little sadistic hellcat on.

So we celebrated by drinking vodka off

of each other. Once I broke out the cocaine, our little party turned into a sex explosion, and we tried every position known to modern man. Hell, we even did some medieval shit. I managed to get audio on most of the ordeal. Some of it on video, but that was a little trickier. But hey, I *am* a professional.

Standing on the balcony in my briefs, I was beginning to realize that at some point I'd need to call Tucker. He'd snap when he heard what his wife was plotting. "Hey, you coming back to bed?" Melissa was insatiable. And I was drained. "No, I'm gonna take my Black ass home." I replied.

I walked back in and started to get dressed. "Well, you are gonna do it aren't ya?" She was starting to annoy me. "Do what?" I groaned, and snorted the last line of coke. "Kill him, goddamn it!" She was getting pissed. "When and where?" I asked. "Tonight. We're going to Akira for dinner around six o'clock. Make it look like a robbery."

Akira was an upscale sushi restaurant in Dearborn. I looked at my watch. 8:57am. "Just have my money ready, I'll be leaving town right afterwards." I snarled as I walked out the door. She followed me out with a puzzled look on her face. "Wait a minute. You're Black?"

I walked past her Rover, and hopped in my silver Audi R8. "You are one smart bitch Melissa. See ya tonight!" I flashed a peace sign, started the engine, and burned rubber out of there.

I had been staying at the Sheraton hotel in Ann Arbor, Michigan, courtesy of Tucker. I decided to go there and shower before breaking the news to him. I got halfway across the Ambassador Bridge when my cell phone rang. It was my partner, Richard Sturm.

"When the fuck are you coming back to Brooklyn?" he shouted, "We're fuckin swamped over here!" Richard could be pretty cool sometimes, but I was loving my time away from him. It was just us and the secretary, Mona at the office. And I was tired of seeing their faces everyday. I did most of the field work, so whenever I got an out of town assignment, it was welcome. "I should be closing the case tonight. I'll let you know." I hung up.

BULLETTIME

Richard's father owned the P.I. office, but he was on an extended leave, recovering from a stroke. In his father's absence, Richard took the reins, and started making business decisions. But he wasn't my boss.

We met in juvie, he was in for assault as well. Since we were both from Queens, we had each other's backs. We didn't give a fuck about that jailhouse segregation shit. Besides, I was always mistaken for Puerto Rican or Middle Eastern anyway. So he had beef with the Whites for hanging out with me, and I had beef with, (you guessed it) everyone.

But he always told me that when we got out of there we'd both have jobs working for his dad's agency in Brooklyn. We'd have to start out answering phones and cleaning the place, but our day would come. It was something to look forward to, even though I was skeptical. But he came through. And once we turned 21, we both became official Private Investigators. I owed him a lot, but I still didn't like him trying to keep tabs on me.

I was starting to lose my buzz and I could feel the hangover growing stronger. I decided to stop in Detroit, and see that mutual friend. He was a bail bondsman who also had the hookup on the best nose candy in Motown. Demetrios Sims. He didn't actually sell coke, but he regularly bonded out a lot of the city's dealers and other devious beings. He'd always work with them on collateral and fees. And in exchange, they'd hook him up with whatever he needed at the time. Mostly electronics, vehicles, and shit like that. He never touched drugs, but he had the right connections.

I pulled into his lot and immediately noticed an unmarked police car. It was a white Impala with government plates. "Fuck," I muttered. "So much for scoring a quick fix." I hopped out of the R8 and strolled casually into the office.

Sims' Bail Bonds. The office was small and stuffy, not unlike any other bail bond office out there. "D, what up!" Demetrios was a relatively small, middle aged Black man. He stood about 5'7, and weighed about 160. But he was as strong as an ox. Plus he knew several differ-

ent Martial Arts. He didn't care much for firearms, he felt that his fist and feet were deadly
enough. He was definitely old school.

I'd known him for a few years, and whenever I
was in town, he'd have me over his house for
barbecues. He and his wife Tracey flew out to
New York for my 23rd birthday party. A real
cool guy. Rumor had it that he was a pimp in
the seventies.

    "Ash! My nigga! What it is, young blood?"
Demetrios' eyes lit up when he saw me, like I
interrupted an uncomfortable situation. There
were two plain clothes cops in his office. One
was a tall, thin Asian, and had a laid back de-
meanor. The other, a stocky White guy, was
sporting a scowl to rival Max Payne's mad-
dened gawk. "I come at a bad time?" I glared at
the cops. "No, not at all, they were just leaving,"
he replied. "Ain't that right, fellas?" Demetrios
seemed irritated by these cops. The White one
started to crack his knuckles. I stepped to Demetrios' side, and crossed my arms.

    Demetrios and I were about the same
height. I was slightly thinner due to the cocaine
diet, but I was just as ready as he was to face off

with these guys. Something about them just didn't seem right. The Asian one grabbed his partner's arm. "Yeah, our business is done here. C'mon, Cross." He pulled the pissed off cop towards the door. Reluctantly exiting the building, the one called 'Cross' stared Demetrios down. "Fuckin' pigs!" Demetrios frowned. "What the fuck was that all about?" I inquired. "Cock suckers are looking for one of my bounty hunters." he said. 'Who, that mother fucker Grey?"

I'd met Ezekiel Grey in Arizona a couple of years back. We collaborated on a case. A real mess involving an exiled member of Yakuza, a psychotic redneck, a suicidal plastic surgeon, and a pair of local radio personalities. An incident I now refer to as 'Bloodlust in the Valley of the Sun'. But that's another story...

"Naw, not EZ," Demetrios chuckled, "a new kid from Naw'lins." I took a seat. "New Orleans, huh? Shit, I was thinking about going out there after this case. Its Mardi Gras right now." I'd never been to Mardi Gras, but on many occasions I'd thought about checking out my hometown. Plus I needed a vacation and figured now was as good a time as ever.

Demetrios sat down at his desk. "Punk ass cops ain't even in their jurisdiction. Motha fuckas is from Miami." I snickered, "Miami? Shit! You should've told those fools to go back to the everglades with that shit!" Demetrios laughed and gave me a fist pound. "So what's up, cool breeze?" He was suddenly back to his jovial self.

I told him the developments in the case he referred to me, sparing him some of the fine details. We had a few laughs, and a few shots of Absolut Vodka he kept stashed in his desk. He gave me the address to a guy on bond with him. A coke dealer named Lil Dane. He told me he'd let Dane know I was coming, and to hook me up.

As I was leaving, I saw the cops' Impala across the street at White Castle. I guess Dunkin' Donuts was too far of a drive. I sped off towards the address.

I pulled up to Lil Dane's house and an adolescent kid ran inside. Obviously, the lookout kid. I started getting second thoughts. I'd

56

been to some fucked up neighborhoods before, hell I'm from the largest housing project in America. But damn, this was one fucked up ghetto. There were four burnt down abandoned houses on the block, bullet holes from multiple drive-bys in almost every house, and no less than three broken down old cars across each lawn.

As I contemplated turning around and getting the fuck out of there, two muscle bound thugs stepped outside of Lil Dane's house. They were both clutching obvious concealed firearms in the front of their pants. They both stood over 6ft and 300lbs. If looks could kill... I stepped out of the R8.

"I'm looking for Lil Dane. Demetrios sent me." The bigger of the two approached me. He had cornrolls that were in desperate need of a rebraid. He was wearing a tank top and had several tattoos, but his complexion was so dark, I couldn't make out what any of the tats were. "Never heard of him." he growled, baring his row of gold teeth. The other guy started to flank towards my right. I smiled, "C'mon, man I'm not a cop or anything. But I do wanna cop some blow. Demetrios from the bail bond company said he'd call."

The cornrolled thug didn't care for my name-dropping. "Look, you fuckin' Arab-" He started. "Arab?" I hated when people mistook me for anything other than what I was. "I'm not a fuckin' Arab, homie, I'm Bi-racial. Do you know what that means?" I demanded. "Yeah, it means confused" he replied, and they both started laughing. I was growing impatient. "I'm half Black, alright? Now get Lil Dane out here. Please." The other one suddenly pulled a gun from his waist. Taurus Millennium 9mm. Handy little pistol, I had one just like it at home. But on this day I was carrying my Heckler & Koch compact .40 caliber in the small of my back. "Maybe you didn't hear the man. Get the fuck outta here before I smoke your half Bi-racial, Black ass!" He pointed the gun at me and chills ran up my spine.

Time slows down when you're staring down the barrel of a gun. Maybe it's just the adrenaline that speeds up your reaction time and makes it seem that way. I don't know. But I've had many guns pulled on me in my lifetime. And it's the same every time. This was no different.

All of a sudden the front door swung open, and out stepped the biggest Puerto Rican I'd ever laid eyes upon. He stood about 6'10", and looked a stout 500lbs. "Chill, niggas," he ordered. The thug lowered his gun. "You Ash?" The biggin grunted. "Yeah, that's me." I sighed with relief. "D just called me. C'mon in."

I proceeded with caution up the broken porch steps and into the house. The look-out kid was in there, along with about six other juveniles. They were listening to classic Mobb Deep, 'Shook Ones pt.2', and taking turns at Madden on a PlayStation 3. They had a blunt rotating, and each one stared me down as I walked in.

I followed the big man to a back room that he made into a makeshift office. He sat down behind the desk. "So you're *Lil* Dane?" I asked. "Yeah. Kinda ironic ain't it? It's like rain… on your wedding day." he grinned. "What? You lost me." I was confused as to what the fuck he was talking about. "Never mind. Just a little inside joke."

I was glad he was in the joking mood. He resembled the late Big Pun only more ferocious look-ing. "How much you need?" He got to the point, which I appreciated. "Two grams. Here's two hun-dred." I stated firmly as I pulled out my wallet. The room filled with the giants' laughter. "Two hundred," he bellowed. "Try three, home boy!" I was stunned. "What? In New York I only pay-" "This aint New fuckin' York, nigga!" He cut me off, and it became very clear to me that he was no longer in a joking mood.

"This is Rock City! Motown, muh fucka! Three hundred or roll the fuck out!" His shouting alerted the two armed thugs outside and they marched in. They stood on either side of me. I started to get a bad feeling so I opened my wallet. I only had $277. "Fuck it, how much for a gram?" It sucks being an addict. "One fitty." Dane seemed to relax a little, but that was about to change.

The muscle head that pulled the gun on me earlier saw my P.I. Badge. He snatched my wallet. "This mutha fucka is a cop!" He yelled and all hell broke loose.

In the blink of an eye, Lil Dane pulled A Benelli semi-automatic shotgun from behind the desk. I knew that if he opened fire with that thing, there would be nothing left of my body to identify. Just chiclets for teeth. I reached behind my back for my HK, and spun completely around so that when I finished the 360, the .40 was pointed at Lil Dane.

I squeezed three rounds off into his face. Red chunks of brain matter shattered the window behind him. The guy on my right almost caved my face in with a powerful left hook that sent me directly to the floor. I slid between the other thug's feet, and without hesitating, I raised the gun to his balls. He howled in pain as I let off four rounds and lifted my leg swiftly enough to kick him backwards. He went down, and I focused on the one who punched me. The one with the cornrolls.

He drew his 9mm and fired nine shots, seemingly in slow motion, as I rolled out of the path of the ensuing bullets. The slugs penetrated the floor, punching holes into the wood, and filling the area with splinters and saw dust. I rolled completely over, feet towards him, back onto my back. I bent my knees so that my feet were flat on the floor as well. I brought the gun between my knees and emptied the clip. Six shots made the guy dance uncontrollably as they hit various body parts. When it was over, his bloodied shell crashed to the floor with a heavy thud. It looked like someone had poured a bucket of red paint on the wall behind him. I ejected the clip, pocketed it, and replaced it with a fresh one.

I jumped to my feet, and crept towards the front room, finger on the trigger. The house was empty. The kids that were hanging out must've left when they heard the shots. Relieved, I hurried back to Lil Dane's office and searched for his supply. I found two Kilos and a wad of cash in his desk. About three grand. I'm sure he had more, but I wasn't greedy. I needed to get the fuck outta Dodge before shit really hit the fan.

I ran back out to the living room only to find myself face to face with the look-out kid. He was pointing a piece of shit Lorcin .380 in my direction. Nuff said. He pulled the trigger and missed. Wide left. His second shot would've probably hit me had the gun not jammed. I was on him like funk on ass. I knocked the gun out of his hand with my gun, and I delivered a solid haymaker to his chin. The punch sent him crashing through the screen door, barely conscious. "Should've picked a better gun" I muttered as I strolled past him and hopped in my ride. Several spectators were gathering outside, so I floored it. I wasn't too worried about the police, knowing they'd take their time responding to a call in this neighborhood. I just didn't want to get lynched by the onlookers.

I got to my hotel and rushed inside. Paranoia had set in and I was trembling. My hands were clammy, and my hangover was in full swing. I decided to get some shut eye before calling Tucker, so I finished some left over Popeye's chicken and laid down. I glanced at my watch. 1:33pm. I'll just take a short nap, I told myself. I've got plenty of time. Just gotta rest a few minutes...

 I awakened to the sound of screaming sirens... 'Holy shit,' I thought. 'They're coming for me!' I jumped up, and ran to the window. It was a fire truck cruising past the hotel. I was relieved, but my heart still felt like it was going to explode. What the fuck time is it? 6:47, Goddamn it! I sliced open one of the bags of blow and did an ungodly line. I smelled like an animal so I hopped in the shower. Minutes later I emerged, ready to close the case. I threw on a Prada shirt, Armani jeans, and some shoes. I don't remember what brand. I holstered the HK, grabbed the tapes of Melissa, and trotted to my vehicle.

 I high tailed it to Akira. The evening air was cold and crisp, and a light layer of snow had fallen. I loved the cold climate. I thought about the day's events and wondered why I ever became a P.I. I would've probably done better as a career criminal. But I liked my job. How I walked the line between right and wrong, yet not quite cross over to either side. Those lines have been blurred for some time now. And I didn't mind a bit. A true antihero, I was just one of many lost souls trying to make my way in this fucked up world. At least that's what I kept telling myself.

I pulled up to Akira around 7:30, tossed the valet my keys and told him to keep it close, I'd be right back. I ran my hand through my hair. A swift wind blew open my shirt like a cape, revealing my tank top underneath. I felt like all eyes were on me as I strolled slowly into the restaurant. I took a look around, and saw various high class types stuffing their faces. Business men and women, ballers, and local television celebrities, all happily chowing down on raw fish, seaweed and rice.

I spotted Tucker and Melissa towards the back of the place. They had just paid for their meal and were getting ready to leave. As I approached their table, Melissa almost went into shock as she noticed me. Like a deer in headlights, her eyes grew wide, as if to say 'No, not here! Wait til we get outside!' Or maybe she had a change of heart, and didn't want Tucker dead anymore.

"What's wrong, Melissa? You look like you just got caught with your pussy open." I loved being an asshole. Tucker leapt out of his chair. "Calibre?! What the hell are you doing here?" He was just as surprised as she was. "Here, take a listen to these tapes.

Not only did the bitch cheat on you, she wanted me to kill you. Tonight." I handed him the tapes. His jaw almost hit the floor. "My office will contact you with your total amount due. You're credit card will be charged within 24hrs." I sneered and winked at Melissa before turning around. She was angry and confused. "You're a fucking bastard!" she shouted. "Tell me something I don't know" I retorted, and exited the place. I returned to the hotel to collect my belongings, and did a couple of lines. After careful consideration, I decided to drive south. Destination: Mardi Gras.

I arrived in New Orleans the next morning. Thank god for my navigation system. I did about a hundred the whole way, only stopping for gas, piss, and to powder my nose. Good coke will keep me going all night, and this was raw uncut shit But I was winding down, and made up my mind to stop at a Motel 6 in East New Orleans. The place was a dive, and I felt right at home. The weary clerk seemed suspicious. That changed when I paid for a week in advance. Room 269. The room smelled stale, it had been a while since it was last rented. I opened the window, cranked the a/c, and hit the sack. "Tonight I'll drink till it hurts." I chuckled, and slipped into a coma-like state for the next 12 hours.

I came to around midnight. I felt refreshed, but hungry as hell. I checked my phone. 12 missed calls. Mostly from Richard, one from Tucker confirming the money transfer, and a few from various broads back in NYC. After hitting the shower, I went to the first eating establishment I saw. A 24hr mom and pop joint called Big Daddy's Kitchen. I feasted on gumbo, okra, and jambalaya. The food was delicious.

After eating to my fill, I headed to Bourbon St. and proceeded to get fucked up. It was Fat Tuesday, the last day of Mardi Gras, and the crowd was enormous. The horseback police tried to maintain order, but it was damn near impossible. I found myself drowning in a drunken sea of frat boys and girls going wild. Beads were flying in all directions and bare tits were everywhere. They came in assorted sizes and colors, and the intoxicated owners were happy to display them in exchange for a cheap necklace of colorful beads. Random fights were breaking out and after about an hour of the chaos, I decided to retreat to a sports bar a few blocks away.

It was a quiet pub called Tiffany's Tavern. The place wasn't crowded, only a couple dozen people were there. I took a seat at the bar and ordered a shot of Stoli. "Nous ne servons pas cela ici! Order something French!" The overworked bartender was extremely thin, and seemed irritated at my ignorance to the fact that the place only served French alcohol. "Ok…? Well in that case get me a Courvoisier."

I looked at the bottles behind the bar. Rows of assorted cognacs, chartreus, guignolets, and other French 'alcoolisees' filled the shelf. "Tenez." He handed me the drink. "Merci." I slammed it. That's when I saw her.

The woman was utterly gorgeous. She had flawless cocoa skin, long brown hair, and the face of an angel. She was wearing a tight black dress, not too formal, but far from sleazy. Her six inch stiletto heels boosted her height to almost six feet. Her perky C-cups sat high above her slim waist. She had a confident look about her, yet seemed sad. She could've been a model for all I knew. Absolutely stunning. But it wasn't until she approached the bar, that I soon realized just who she was.

"Hey Pierre, how we doing tonight?" She asked in a sweet sounding voice. The bar-

tender's eyes lit up. "Bien, Tiffany, tres bien.
Alize Bleu?" She took a seat next to me.
"Please." She smiled. "You got it!" he scrambled to make the drink. I saw this as a prime
opportunity to pounce. "Tiffany's Tavern. You
wouldn't happen to be *that* Tiffany would
you?" I wanted to keep it casual, without pro-
jecting my attraction to her. She smiled, "Yes,
this is my bar. I'm Tiffany L'Croix." Beautiful
smile. Perfect teeth. "Ash Calibre. Nice to
meet you." She shook my hand. Her skin was
butter soft.

We struck up a conversation, and
grabbed a table. She had the bartender bring
over a bottle of Louis XIII. On the house, of
course. We chatted for about an hour before I
asked her what was troubling her. She said her
sister Celeste had run off with a member of
some biker gang from Mississippi. The
Wraiths.

Her sister had just turned 17, still a mi-
nor, and Tiffany was her legal guardian. They
had different dads, and their mother was dead.
She killed Celeste's father and herself one night
after a drunken argument.

Tiffany's father was the original owner of the bar, but he signed it over to Tiffany, and moved to Paris. Tiffany juggled running the bar, attending college, and taking care of her sister. Celeste had been through a lot, and Tiffany just wanted her to be happy. But she'd been hanging with the wrong crowd. Hell, everyone does at some point. The drugs, the guns, the crime sprees. It all sounded too familiar. But this crowd could get her killed. The Wraiths had achieved notoriety throughout the Gulf Coast as a gang not to be fucked with.

When Tiffany tried to reason with Celeste, the little rebel took off with her boyfriend, a member of the gang. That was a week ago. She hadn't heard from her since. I told Tiffany I'd help anyway I could, and showed her my credentials. Elated, she immediately hired me to locate Celeste. It was getting late, so she invited me to her place for further conversation regarding my new case. I followed her there, hoping for more than conversation.

Tiffany owned a four bedroom house in a pretty decent neighborhood. It was just her and her sister living there. Her dad stayed in the guest room whenever he came to town, about every six months. We were greeted at the door by her rottweiler, Shane. I didn't really like dogs, but I made an exception for her.

We stayed up most of the night getting to know each other, and discussing the details of the case. We had a lot in common, she was bi-racial as well. Her father was Creole, and her mother was White. She was two years younger than me, and was getting her BA in psychology. Which I thought was awesome, seeing as how mentally screwed up I was.

She informed me that the Wraiths were responsible for nearly one third of the crime in the Gulf area. They allegedly had a number of cops in their ranks. Finding Celeste wasn't going to be an easy task, but I didn't care. I was smitten. We didn't even discuss a fee. It didn't matter to me. There was just something about Tiffany. We finished a bottle of Moet and started to get cozy by the fireplace.

I tried to make a move but she wasn't having it. "I'm sorry, but I just don't get down like that. I don't know you that well yet." she said. I had to respect that, so I backed off. Besides, she did say 'yet'. It only made me want her more.

"Are you ok to drive?" she asked. If she only knew. "If not, then you can stay in the guest room tonight. But you better behave. Shane is trained to castrate on command." I chuckled, but she looked dead serious, which made me slightly nervous. She showed me to the guest room and kissed me goodnight. On the cheek, but I was happy with that. She smelled like a dozen roses.

Unable to sleep, I started going over my plan to find Celeste. I went into her bedroom, and took a look around. It was a dark, gothic looking room, cluttered with black leather and red lace clothing. Not what I figured a typical teenage girl's room would look like. There were no Boy Band posters on these walls, just bands like Atreyu, Aiden, HIM, and AFI.

I went through her belongings and gathered useful items. Pictures of her and her boyfriend Thomas, notes from friends, shit like that. I got on her iMac, and started looking for information on The Wraiths. Where they hung out, what they were about, anything that would help. I couldn't hack into her email, but I checked her browsing history. She frequented a Wraith owned website.

There I found out that they owned Iron Cross Casino in Bay St. Louis, and Club Darqcyde in Gulfport, both in Mississippi. I looked at the time. 6am. Might as well get an early start. I left Tiffany a note, thanking her for her hospitality and assuring her that I'd do everything I could to locate Celeste. I wrote down my cell phone number and headed out. First stop, my motel room for a shower, a change of clothes, and some sugar booger.

I felt ready for the world. I was down to my last clean set of clothes: Black Fendi suit, white shirt, and a tie. I looked official, but I needed a haircut. Fuck it, I pulled it back into a ponytail. It was old school, but it worked. My phone rang. It was Richard.

"Hey, good job on the Tucker case. I got another one for you. Its local, did you get my messages or what?" I broke the news to him that I was on another case. "Bullshit! What case?" He was getting irate. "It just came up last night. I'm in New Orleans. I'm looking for this girl." "Yeah, I'll bet you're looking for a girl! Here's the deal, you've got two days to do whatever it is you're doing out there. Then get your ass back-" "Fuck that!" I interrupted. "Don't ever fuckin' talk to me like that! I told you I'm on a case. I'll be back when I'm done here."

Recognizing that I was pissed, Richard changed his tone. "Look, man, I'm not trying to be a dick ok? We're partners, bro. I know I'm not your boss. But for now I've gotta fill in for the old man. And I can't run this office if I'm in the field, doing your job, while you're out of town doing God knows what. Now we've got several local cases pending. And I need your help. Take the rest of the week, finish up whatever it is you're doing, and *please* get back here by next Monday. Ok?" Not good enough. "I'll come back to New York when the case is over. I'll email you later with the specifics" I retorted. He sighed, "Fine, but please hurry."

I hung up the phone. I hated being

told what to do. Especially by someone with no authority over me.

My first stop of the day: Celeste's boyfriend's last known address. It was in the Riggs Trailer Park, one of the city's many eyesores. As with many areas in New Orleans, you could still see the aftermath of Katrina's wrath. But something told me that this place looked pretty fucked up before the hurricane.

I pulled up to his trailer and was immediately confronted by two large pit bulls. The dogs seemed to be starving, and I must've looked like a bowl of Purina One to them. I honked the horn, and a man in his late thirties appeared at the window. He came outside and got the devil dogs to go inside the trailer.

"Thanks," I said as I stepped out the car. He frowned, "You from CPS?" He was a typical redneck, filthy overalls, no shirt, and bare feet. The few teeth he had left were nearly black, and his face was stained with grease or something.

"No." I replied. "The ASPCA?" "No." "The Po-leese?" "Not exactly." I reluctantly smiled. The stench of dog shit and body odor was almost overpowering. "Then just who the hell are ya, exactly?" He was getting agitated, and I was getting sick. "I'm looking for Thomas J. Harwell. He lives here, right?" The man scratched his head. "Who wants to know?" He glanced at the barking dogs in the window.

"Look, he's dating my niece, Celeste. I just got in town and wanted to say hello. I figured she'd be with Thomas. She told me about him, hell, she talks about him all the time. Is he around?" He wasn't buying it my bullshit.

"Tommy don't live here no mo! So you gosta leave. Go on now, git!" He turned and started marching to the door. I started to follow him, but stopped halfway. "Hey wait, I've got a few questions." He got to the door, flipped me off, and opened it, unleashing the Hounds of Hell upon me. They charged at me one after the other, fangs eagerly anticipating the long awaited meal.

As the first one leapt up towards my face, I grabbed the HK. When his front paws made contact with my chest, I began a back flip. His mouth was a mere inch from mine, as we went horizontal while airborne. I was completely upside down when the shots rang out. My head was a few feet from the ground and my feet were straight up, above me. The beast let out a high pitched yelp as two .40 caliber slugs entered his body, devastating his organs and spilling them out through the exit wounds.

Completing the back flip, I landed on my right knee and left foot. The dead dog landed between my legs, on his back. His tongue was extended, and his eyes glazed over. I raised the gun just as the other beast was upon me. Only time for one shot, but it went in his mouth and severed his spine on the way out the back of his neck. The dog was killed instantly, but his momentum sent him crashing into me, knocking me backwards, and causing me to smack my head on the concrete. The impact rendered me unconscious.

I was only out for a few seconds, but when I came to, the redneck was standing over me, holding *my* gun. "Now, you pet murderin' so'ma bitch, Its yo turn ta die!" He spat into my face and pointed the gun. "You gonna take the safety off first?" I bluffed. He turned the gun to the side, and looked at it. I struck promptly, delivering a powerful kick to his balls. He let out a squeal, and I was on my feet instantly. I unloaded a half dozen punches to his face and gut, and followed up with a crushing elbow to the chin. He was out before he hit the ground.

"Get away from my dad, mother fucker!" A rough looking kid appeared at the door armed with a sawed off shotgun. I dropped to the ground, grabbed my gun and took aim at the kid. "I've got no problem killing a kid! Especially if you're related to this fuck! I'll probably just be doing you a favor! Are you Thomas?" I yelled. "No. Tommy aint here! He's in Gulfport."

The kid started to cry. He couldn't have been older than 12. "Alright, put down the gun, and let's talk." He lowered the shottie. Progress. Suddenly, there was a raspy southern voice behind me. "Now you put the gun down, mister. Nice and slow." I turned my head to see two cops behind me, guns drawn.

Interrogations. Cross Examinations. Recorded conversations. These are things I conducted regularly in my line of work. But sometimes I ended up on the receiving end. And for the next two hours that's what I had to endure. They let me make my phone call which I used to call Tiffany and tell her to come down. Then it was back to the questioning. Who was I? What was my business in New Orleans? Why did I just kill two dogs? The cops finally eased up when Tiffany arrived at the station to vouch for me.

They knew Tiffany, and were familiar with her situation with Celeste. They even stopped into her bar on occasion. They seemed like decent cops, not under the umbrella of the Wraiths, but they still wanted to find something to charge me with. Everything I did at the trailer park was in self defense, so they were just fishing for information at that point. So Tiffany offered them free drinks for a month, and they happily returned my firearm and released me.

My suit was stained with doggy blood, so Tiffany took me shopping. She said I needed to blend in more, as I looked like a cop in that suit. I personally didn't know very many cops who dressed as well as I did, but I let her buy me few days' worth of casual type clothes. I changed into a pair of blue True Religion jeans a black Affliction t-shirt, and black Dior Homme sneakers.

We had lunch, and I decided to get back on the hunt. I went to Dirty Charlie's Motorcycle Shop and asked around. "What you say your name was?" A hefty, oil stained mechanic asked. "Ash Calibre" I replied. "Any relation to Lamont Calibre?" The name sounded slightly familiar. "I don't think so. Why, who is he?" I asked, puzzled. The grease monkey scratched his head. "Oh, just some dead guy. I do maintenance part-time at a graveyard. He was buried there a couple of nights ago. The name Calibre isn't very common, so I thought...well never mind. Anyway, sorry I can't help you." I started to get a funny feeling in the pit of my stomach, but then realized it was just gas so I ripped one.

"Thanks anyway," I nodded as I started to walk away. "Hey, what cemetery was it? Maybe I'll pay my respects. You never know right?" "Saint Jo's up on Washington," He wrinkled his nose, "Hey, did you fart?" I hit the door and walked briskly to my car.

I hate cemeteries. The irony is that I've sent plenty of people there. Mostly in the line of work, but again, sometimes that line gets blurred. As I drove to the cemetery I tried to remember who Lamont was. I knew I was related to him, but I couldn't exactly place the name. I thought hard. I recalled seeing his name on envelopes, so I knew he wrote letters to my mother. 'Think...think...From Lamont and Ebony Calibre'. Holy shit! My grandparents. So this Lamont was my mother's estranged father.

I pulled up to the cemetery, got out and started reading tombstones. So many graves. So many forgotten souls. I walked around for a half hour and was about to give up when I came across the headstone. 'Reverend Lamont Calibre, loving husband and father 1943-2008'. "Loving, huh? Yeah right" I said out loud. I couldn't help but feel slightly content that he was dead. Hell, he wanted me dead before I was even born. So fuck him.

"Did you know Lamont?" A soft female voice startled me. I turned around to see a frail woman in her forties smiling at me. "No, not at all" I mumbled and started to walk away. "That's too bad," She sighed. "He was a good man. He was my father." I stopped in my tracks. "Your father?" I began to realize who the woman was. "Yeah. I miss him so much." She started to weep. "So you're Christina." I sneered and approached her.

My mother used to tell me stories about her evil older sister. The one who tried to make her drink Drano when she refused to abort me. The one who smacked her in the stomach while she was asleep, eight months pregnant. The one who showed me no love when I was born, referring to me as 'the devil's son'.

"Yes my name is Christina. But...do I know you?" I could hear the fear in her voice, as she watched my fists clench. I wanted to punch her right in the face for the emotional pain she caused my mother. I was starting to turn red with anger. "Oh my god... Ash?!" she blurted as my eyes started to water. I fought back the tears. "Yeah, and I know all about you, bitch!"

I never was good at controlling my emotions. "Ash, whatever Sheri told you about me...well...was probably true. And I'm sorry for that. But I was a troubled youth. I'm nothing like that now. I'm an active member in my church-" I didn't want to hear the bullshit. "The same church that appointed *this* man a reverend?" I spat at Lamont's headstone. "After he turned his back on his teenage daughter, when she needed support the most, and drove her down a fateful path?"

The anger I had suppressed for so long was building back up. But I was especially angry at myself. That, coupled with the guilt for my own role in my mother's demise was unbearable. But I had faced those demons on many occasions. And it damn near drove me insane. But here and now, I was angry at Christina.

"Ash, I tried numerous times to visit you and Sheri, but she wouldn't allow it. But my parents wrote her letters, and sent her money every month. I loved my sister, and I'm so sorry about what happened to her, but don't walk away from the only family you've got left." This angered me even more. "You don't know a fucking thing about me! The only family I've ever had is dead! So you can go to hell with your hypocrite father. And when you get there mention my name. You'll get a discount." I turned around and started to leave.

"Ash, wait! Just please come to church services with me tonight. There's someone you need to meet." "Yeah, who's that, Jesse Jackson or Al Sharpton?" I scoffed and flipped my hair back. "No. It's your father" she said and I suddenly felt like throwing up.

I faced her once again, only this time she was a blurred rendition of herself. "Wh-What did you say?" I started to get dizzy, and everything was starting to go dark. "First Kings 8:50 says, 'You must forgive those who sinned against you and forgive their transgressions'. Your father, Aaron Davis, served his time and found god while he was in prison. When he got out, he repented for

the sins he committed. He begged for for-
giveness, and reached out to our family. He
became a regular at our church, and got bap-
tized. He is a minister now." And with that, I
passed out.

When I came to, I was surrounded by
paramedics trying to revive me. "Sir, did you
take any drugs, alcohol, or medication today?" A female EMT asked. "Who…me?
Never touch the stuff." I groaned and stood
up.

"You need to relax, and let us help
you." she said sternly. "I'm fine, besides I
don't have insurance." I sighed. I was lying,
but I didn't want to deal with the bullshit involved with a hospital visit. "Ash, you should
listen to them." It was Christina. She was
standing by the ambulance trying to look
concerned. "Don't you fucking tell me what
to do!" I yelled. My head was killing me, and
I had to get out of there. "Well you really
should come to church tonight." The persis-
tent woman handed me a flyer for her
church.

'Heaven's Gate Baptist Church' up on

Monroe. I shot her a dirty look, crumpled the flyer, and tossed it to the ground. I flipped her off, and stumbled to my car. The EMTs tried to stop me, but I didn't care. The only thing I needed was my self prescribed nasal medication, so I headed back to the hotel.

After doing a few lines, I sat and thought about my new dilemma. I couldn't believe my mother's family was cool with her rapist now. I had to confront them. No, I needed to kill *him*. Confused and angry, I started to pace the room. My phone rang. It was Tiffany, wondering if I wanted to have dinner with her. As much as I wanted to spend more time with her, I declined the offer, telling her I'd be checking the leads in Gulfport later that night, and I had some other business to take care of first. Sounding slightly disappointed, she wished me luck and hung up.

I cleaned my gun, and changed clothes. Black hoodie, black jeans, and black steel toe boots. Realizing exactly what needed to be done, I did another line and left the room.

There was a public computer in the lobby, so I logged onto the City of New Orleans public records website. Aaron Davis was a registered sex offender so his picture was posted. He was fifty five, and looked hardened. I saw familiarity in his face. There was an obvious resemblance. The gray eyes, the jet black hair. But I also saw evil in his face. Maybe 'Christina was right,' I thought, 'maybe I am the devil's son.' I cleared the internet history on the computer, and headed to Heaven's Gate.

I parked across the street from the church, with full view of the parking lot. The lot was well lit, and I made use of my binoculars. The lot was filling quickly, and it wasn't long before Aaron arrived alone in a Ford Edge. I got a good look at his rugged face. Definitely him.

I waited until church was in session, put on some gloves, and jogged across the street. I jimmied the door and climbed into the back seat. I laid down on the floor and waited. I thought about what I was getting ready to do, and my mind went numb.

I've killed before. For the job, for greed, and for self preservation. But this was different. This was the man who did the unspeakable. The man who raped a teenage girl, and ruined her life. But it was also the man who gave me life. Chills ran up and down my spine while I waited.

About an hour later, he got in the car. I waited until he exited the lot, and I put the gun to his head. "Don't turn around!" I warned, and he almost swerved into the next lane. "What's going on?" He asked, bewildered. "Shut the fuck up, I'll tell you where to go. Just keep your eyes on the road!" I commanded. I directed him to a swamp a few miles away, on the outskirts of town.

"Get out!" I shoved his head forward. We stepped out the car and I made him face me. He saw the resemblance as well. "Christina said you were in town. You're Sheri's son right? My son-" I hit him across the face hard with the gun, knocking him off balance, and he fell to his knees. Blood gushed from his shattered nose, ruining his cheap suit "Call me your 'son' again. Do it again! I fucking dare you," I yelled. "In fact, say my mother's name again, you piece of shit! Say it again!" He tried to stand up, but I shoved him back down. "Stay on your knees, where you belong!" "Please, I've paid for my crimes. I'm a man of God now." He begged. "Maybe God can forgive you.

But I can't." I put the gun to his head. "Wait! If it wasn't for me, there would be no you! Think about that!" He was panicking, glancing around the area. Maybe for a passerby, maybe for something to use as a weapon.

"I've thought about it. You made me. And now you're gonna be killed by me. You think about *that*." He raised his hands and pled, "I gave you life and now you're taking mine? You don't have to do this." "I know I don't. But I want to. I've just got one question. Why'd you rape her?" He started to sob. "I wasn't right in the head back then, I've been seeing a shrink for years now, and I'm better. But back then… I dunno, I just saw her one day and she was so beautiful. I couldn't get her off my mind. I fell in love. I wanted to give her the world. I didn't want it to turn out the way it did. I-I just-" "I'm so tired of hearing that bullshit," I roared. "She was a kid, you sick fuck!" I kicked him in the mouth, sending him back into the swamp. He emerged a few seconds later, spitting out blood, water, and shattered teeth. He choked on his words, "Look, I'm sorry. I've always regretted what I did."

The rage was building uncontrollably inside me. "Fuck you! You destroyed her! An innocent girl!

She's dead because of you!" I kicked him again, this time connecting with the side of his left eye. I heard a crunch and he let out a short scream. He fell back into the water, holding his face. "Get up," I demanded, and pulled him out of the swamp. It was then I realized that I had shattered his eye socket, and the sight of his left eye hanging out of his face gave me pleasure. Barely conscious, he started to pray. "Though I walk through the valley of the shadow of death…" The fury boiled over and I started pulling the trigger. I kept firing until the loud bangs were replaced by sharp clicks, as I kept trying to shoot with an empty gun.

Eight headshots, and five to the chest, all at point blank range. The bullets disintegrated his face and turned his head into one huge crater, spilling his liquefied brains into the bayou. The chest shots did the same to his heart. The bloody carnage was not a sight for the faint of heart.

The whole process disturbed a few nearby gators, who seemed to take interest in the gaping carcass. I backed away from the body and watched as the gators closed in on it. It didn't take long before they tore Aaron limb from limb. I watched the hungry reptiles feast on the body. I then put his vehicle in neutral and pushed it into the swamp. I turned and started to run. I ran for about a mile, when it started to rain. Not hard, just a light sprinkle, but a flash of lighting hinted at heavier rain to come. I flagged down a cab and had him drop me off a few blocks from my car.

I don't remember the last time I cried. But as I sat in my car, listening to the rain get heavier, I wept thoroughly for about ten minutes. I tried to clear my head, but I was an emotional wreck. I had imagined killing that man many times before. I hated him for what he'd done. But now that he was dead, I felt no satisfaction. Only more pain. I drove to a liquor store and bought a fifth of Jack Daniels. I drank half the bottle before heading towards Gulfport.

In the hour or so it took me to get to Gulfport, the weather went from rain to extremely foggy. I had never in my life seen fog as thick as it was that night. I had a good buzz going, and trying to drive, focus on navigation, and drink was damn near impossible. When I started to get drowsy, I cursed myself for not bringing my powdered energy booster. I drove past Iron Cross Casino in Bay St. Louis. I figured I'd stop there in the morning. I wanted to check out this Club Darqcyde first. I started thinking about the days events when I dozed off.

I was awakened by my head bouncing off of the steering wheel, and a huge splash as my car landed in the Gulf of Mexico. I looked up to see the bridge I had just driven off of. "Shit.. *shit*!" I panicked as water rushed through my open windows, filling the R8. I struggled to get out of the car as it sank like a boulder. I thrashed around aimlessly, as my recurring nightmare was suddenly becoming reality. I managed to clamber through the window, and was just above my car, following it deeper into the abyss. I sucked in the murky water as I gave a last ditch effort to get back up to the surface. No luck. My arms were just flailing about violently. I felt fatigue start to set in, and I knew I was in trouble. I gulped for air, but instead, got nothing but water. This was the end. I thought to myself, 'I guess I'll be seeing my father a lot sooner than I thought'. I don't think either one of us would be missed very much. Fuck it, I'd kill him again in Hell if I got the chance. My body stopped moving and began to succumb to the darkness.

Not yet. A shadowy figure suddenly appeared above me. He swam quickly to me, taking hold of me and pulling me to the surface. "Breathe, damn it!" he ordered and I complied, coughing wildly in the process. He towed me to dry land and pulled me out of my near grave. I proceeded to puke my guts out onto the road. Thick yellow and brown liquid shot from my mouth and nose so violently, I thought my head would explode. I began to pull myself together after a few minutes.

"Thanks, man." I whispered, between gasps for air. "You're lucky we saw you." a man said. "There aren't any other cars around. We just happened to see your headlights take a nosedive off that bridge. You shouldn't be in this fog if you can't drive in it." he scolded. "Yeah, I know. But I'm on a job." I said and looked up to see two familiar faces.

It was the two cops from Demetrios' office. They looked like they had both been in a fight. The White one was soaked and shivering, my obvious savior. The Asian one recognized me. "Hey, do I know you?" I slowly stood up. "No. But we saw each other at Sims' Bail Bonds. What the fuck are you guys doing out here?" I asked, puzzled at the coincidence. "We're on a job too," the White one replied, "and we're losing time. Let's go." They started to walk towards their car. I followed. "Hey…its Cross, isn't it? Hey, I appreciate you saving my ass, but my car is gone, bro. Can I get a ride?" I asked. "We're headed in the opposite direction," he grunted as they got in the Impala, and disappeared into the fog.

 Wondering what their hurry was, I remembered Demetrios telling me they were looking for a New Orleans Bounty Hunter. 'Good luck finding *anyone* in this fog', I thought as I glanced at my watch. Midnight.

 It was a cold night, and my water logged clothes and inebriated state made the situation uncomfortable. I ran to keep warm, and when I got to a gas station I went inside and used the hand dryer in the bathroom. My hair smelled like a wet dog. My HK was still intact, I wasn't too worried about it getting wet, HK's are known for taking a great deal of abuse and maintaining their reliability. I was going to miss my car, though.

 After about twenty minutes under the dryer, I bought two Red Bulls and asked the clerk for directions. "Darqcyde? Shit, it's about a half mile east of here. You sure you wanna go there, though?" I gulped down the energy drinks and ran out the door towards the club. I didn't know if Celeste would be there or not, but someone there had to know something. The adrenaline was kicking in as I approached my destination.

 But when I arrived, there were four police

cars and an ambulance outside, and I could hear more sirens on the way. A helicopter hovered above, as paramedics were trying to lift a body off of a row of fallen motorcycles. I quickly flashed my badge at a young officer and asked what happened. "A fuckin' massacre, that's what. Several dead inside. Including a couple of kids." He answered solemnly and my heart almost jumped out of my chest. Passing by a corpse outside, I made my way inside, pushing my way past the officers. What I saw resembled a slaughterhouse. The carnage rivaled anything I'd ever seen.

Body bags were being brought in, and a detective was just about place a white sheet over a young woman's body when everything seemed to slow down. I suppose it was the shock setting in, as I started to realize that Celeste just may be dead. I walked over to the body, and shoved the detective when he tried to stop me. I gazed into her face and confirmed it was Celeste L'Croix, dead from three gunshot wounds. I also saw her boyfriend, Thomas J. Harwell, lying dead a few feet from her.

Wondering what I was going to tell Tiffany, I stepped outside for fresh air. That's when I overheard an officer say the shooter was DOA a couple of miles up the road. Once again, I broke into a sprint. I had to see who was responsible for this bloodbath, even if he was dead. Blinded by the fog, I kept running until I saw the flashing blue and red lights. I came upon a deadly accident involving a Hummer and an unidentifiable burning SUV. A fire truck was just arriving to put out the blaze. A man had been ejected during the collision, and I approached the officer standing over him.

"This is a crime scene. Back off, he commanded. Panting for breathe I said "Its ok, I'm with you guys," and I showed him my badge. "Private Investigator? Get the fuck outta here!" He grabbed my arm, but not before I got a look at the dead man on the pavement. I recognized the bloodied, disfigured face, but barely. It was Ezekiel Grey, the best bounty hunter in the business. We worked together before, and although we didn't quite see eye to eye, seeing his broken, lifeless body on the ground was gut wrenching. "I know this man," I mumbled. I felt like throwing up. Again.

Wiping the sweat from my forehead, I couldn't believe the day I was having. But I took comfort in knowing that if Ezekiel shot those people in the bar, it was with good reason. He'd been in the business for a long time, and he wasn't known for making mistakes.

But I guess this one cost him his life.

"Was he a friend of yours?" a muffled voice came from behind me. It was an older man, with blood all over his Versace suit. He was being treated by paramedics. "Not exactly, why?" I asked. "He died in my arms. I-I just-couldn't see his vehicle in the fog. I'm sorry. I-killed-him," he started sobbing. Without a second thought, I threw a right uppercut to his face. It connected with his chin, and he folded like a chair. He was out cold. "You're under arrest, boy," an officer said as he pulled out his cuffs. "That's the former mayor of Biloxi you just punched." I couldn't care less. After the day I just had, nothing could faze me.

At the station, I was allowed to make a phone call. I decided to call Demetrios to do a pre-bond. Also, since he and Ezekiel were friends, I felt I should be the one who told him what happened. When he didn't answer his cell, I tried his home phone. His wife Tracey answered. She sounded terrible, like she had been crying. "Sorry for waking you Tracey. It's Ash. I need to speak to D." I said. She spoke softly, and slowly. "I wasn't asleep, Ash. I guess you didn't hear. Demetrios was killed today." I dropped the phone.

I must've blacked out because the next thing I remembered was lying in a hospital bed. I opened my eyes to see a very sad Tiffany L'Croix sitting in a chair beside me. "How long was I out?" I moaned. Her bloodshot eyes lit up when she heard my voice. "Two days. Stress induced coma. Um…they said there was a lot of cocaine in your system too." She paused long and seemed to be struggling to fight back tears.

"Look, you did everything you could to find my sister, and I thank you from the bottom of my heart. And you're welcome to stay at my house while you get better. How are you feeling?"

I wanted to tell her that I could've prevented her sister's death, had I not been hellbent on killing Aaron Davis. Hell, if I hadn't been drinking, and driven off that bridge, I probably would've made it in time to save her. I wanted to tell her that she was the last person I expected to see at my side, but the only person I wanted to be there. But as I gazed into her eyes, all I could say was "Take me home."

BULLETTIME

<u>Hell To Pay</u>

Time slows down when you're staring down the barrel of a gun. For some people, it's just for a few seconds. For others, it slows down long enough for their whole lives to flash before their eyes. And for a slight few, time slows down just enough to allow for a swift reaction, giving that person a slight advantage. I believe it's different for everyone. This phenomenon is commonly referred to as 'Bullet Time'.

Revenge. Payback. Retribution. These words clouded my mind as I arrived at the emergency room. "Nikki Jackson's room please!" I demanded of the receptionist, as I brushed past the line of sick and injured people lining up to wait for help. "Sir you'll have to wait in line." She responded without looking up. I stuck my badge in her face. "I won't ask again," I fired back. "Oh- uhhh...," her hands scrambled across the computer's keyboard. "Room 313." I turned and marched to the elevator.

As I reached the 3rd floor and approached my sister's room, my cell phone rang. It was Sam Kusinagi, my partner. "Yeah," I answered. "Cross, how is she?" He asked. "I'm headed to her room now, I'll call you back." I hung up and entered the room. "Vinny!" My sister shrieked happily at the sight of me. I immediately hugged her. She had two black eyes and was wearing a cast on her right arm.

"Mom's on her way. What happened?" I asked calmly. "They took him, Vinny! They took him!" "Took who? What the fuck happened?" I was getting irritated by her lack of

102

clarity. She started to cry, which made me more upset. I sat down. "Did Chris do this? You know, I never did approve of you marrying that Black-" "Vinny!" She loudly interrupted. "He didn't do this, so don't talk about him like that!"

They'd been married for four years, which is longer than anyone in my family thought they'd last. Hell, that was longer than both my marriages combined. Still, I didn't like the guy. And it wasn't because of his race, I wasn't racist, just overprotective, I guess. Maybe a little prejudiced as well, but there's a huge difference.

My problem with Chris was his past. He'd been locked up twice for selling crack. When he met Nikki, he told her that he was done with that lifestyle. And as far as I knew, he kept straight for the six years they'd been together. They got married and had two kids. But they had a hard time making ends meet. There were just not a lot of employers who wanted an ex-con on their payroll. He worked temporary jobs here and there, but nothing steady. I helped them out as well, and they were getting by.

But then he told her that his problems would soon be over. Said he just needed to take a trip to Canada, and he'd come back wealthy. Turns out he was trying to transport a pound of cocaine to Toronto, but didn't quite make it. He got pulled over in Detroit for speeding. The cops searched his car and viola! Trafficking charge. Knowing Chris was facing some serious time, Nikki used a bondsman in Detroit to bail him out. Then she brought him back to Miami, which was a violation of the bond.

"He was gonna make the court date. They didn't give him a chance! Those bounty hunters kicked in the door. He started fighting them because he didn't want the kids to see... They tazed him and I tried to help him. But this big, Hillbilly mother fucker pushed me down the stairs. My nose is broken, Vin! And my arm is fractured. They didn't even check to see if I was ok. They just took him. In front of the kids, Vinnyyy!" She broke down again and I tried to console her. But I could feel the anger building up inside of me. They had no right. Arresting Chris was one thing, but hurting my family? They crossed the line. "I'll take care of it," I told her. "Now tell me about this big, Hillbilly mother fucker."

He worked for Sims' Bail Bonds in Detroit. "Sam! You down to take a road trip to Motown?" I wasn't exactly sure what I was going to do, once I got there. I didn't want to get an out of state felony. But I wanted to break this guy's face. Either way, I knew that I'd probably need backup. I'd just gotten off the phone with my Captain, informing him that I'd be taking the rest of the week off. Now I just needed to convince Sam to do the same. It wasn't hard once I told him the situation.

"No one fucks with my partner's family. Yeah, let's get this son of a bitch!" I knew I could count on Sam. We had been partners in the Miami-Dade Police Department for twelve years, and he'd always had my back regardless of whether I was right or wrong. He was fresh out of the Academy when he was assigned to me. This was a month after my first partner took a 12guage to the midsection at close range, splitting him in half.

Sam and I didn't really get along at first,

I felt like no one could replace my partner. But eventually we became best friends. Now there was no one who I'd rather be paired up with. A mild mannered fellow, he moved to Miami from Tokyo when he was ten. He had a strict upbringing, but it instilled values in him that are lacking in many of today's youth. Honor and loyalty were very important to him. And I trusted him with my life.

I told Sam to pack a couple of throw-away guns, and some trip supplies. I assured my sister that everything would be ok, and went home to pack. We left that afternoon, around three pm. We took turns driving our unmarked police car, an '07 Impala. I alternated between Rockstar energy drinks, and bottles of Asahi beer, courtesy of Sam.

"What guns did you bring?" I slurred as my buzz kicked in. "Those two Beretta nines we took off those Cuban bangers last week. Plus the pistol grip Mossberg we got from Ray-Ray." Ray-Ray was a small time arms dealer in Miami. We allowed him to do business, as long as he didn't sell to kids. In return, he kept us informed about various crimes in the area. He also hooked us up with weapons from time to time. "I brought my Glock too, and plenty of ammo," he added. "Good," I replied. "I've got my M2, but I don't plan on using it. One of those nines will do just fine." I loved my Sig Mauser M2, but I used it for work. And I didn't want anything traced back to me. But the nines were dirty, serial numbers scraped off, untraceable.

We arrived in Detroit the following morning, around ten am. We drove straight to Sims' Bail Bonds. I felt grimy from the drive, and didn't smell too good, but I was anxious to meet these bounty hunters.

The office was a tired looking shit hole, just like the rest of the city. But I liked shit holes. In a city like this, a crime could go un-solved for quite some time. Hell, it wasn't uncommon for me to be assigned to a crime that *I* committed in Miami. I'd either pin it on some low life piece of shit, or I'd deem it as unsolved and lose the file. But this was a differ-ent city. The Motor City. Rock City. Motown. The D. And I wasn't quite sure what my limita-tions were here, but I was going to find out.

As we stepped into the office, a middle aged Black man entered from the back room. "How can I help you?" he smiled. "You the owner?" I snarled. "Yeah, I'm Demetrios Sims. This is my company. And *you* are?" He took a seat behind the front desk. "I'm Detective Cross. This is my partner, Sergeant Kusinagi. We're investigating an assault in Miami by one of your bounty hunters. A big, Hillbilly mother fucker." I was straight to the point. "Assault?" he chuckled, "My guys don't assault people. If, in the process of doing their job, the subject puts up a fight, they will fight back and restrain the subject." "Does that include pushing an unarmed woman down a fucking flight of stairs?!" I was showing my anger, which I didn't want to do just yet.

But the lack of sleep, coupled with the growing hangover I was experiencing, had me in no mood for his vindictive tone. "What agency did you guys say you're from?" His smile was replaced with a slight frown. "Cause I need to see some badges right now!" I reluctantly showed him my badge. "Miami P.D. huh?" he said dryly. "This conversation is over. Come back with Detroit P.D. and maybe we'll talk. Until then, don't let the door hit you on the way out."

I clenched my fists, and just then the door flew open. "D, what up?" A medium built pretty boy entered the office. He looked like he could use a haircut, and smelled like pussy and beer. I couldn't tell what race he was, maybe an Arab or something. But he slightly resembled Prince.

"Ash! My nigga! What it is young blood?" Sims smiled. "I come at a bad time?" the kid asked as he sized me up. "No, not at all." Sims replied, "They were just leaving. Right gentlemen?" I cracked my knuckles. I was ready to start kicking ass. That's what I came here for. To kick ass and get answers. But Sam grabbed my arm. "Yeah, our business is done here. C'mon, Cross." He pulled me towards the door. I hoped Sims knew this wouldn't be our last encounter.

"Goddamn it, I'm gonna kill him!" We sat in the car for a few minutes while I vented. "That cocky son of a bitch!" I pounded the dash with my fist. Sam remained composed.

"Calm down, man. We'll catch up to him later. We've got plenty of time. But right now I'm hungry. And White Castle's across the street."

He drove over to White Castle, and we grabbed a window booth. He devoured sliders like a wild beast consuming a fresh kill. The sight of it made me sick to my stomach. I went to the bathroom and splashed my face. My head was killing me. I dug into my pocket, and pulled out a handful of Percosets. I swallowed two, and put the rest back in my pocket. Sam didn't know about my pill habit, and he didn't need to know. I wasn't addicted, I just popped a few pills now and then. Percosets, Oxy, Vicodin, shit like that. It helped ease the pain of being me.

"The pretty boy left." Sam was finishing off his food as I returned to the booth. "What?" I grumbled, as I sat down. "The pretty boy at the Bail Bonds place. He just drove off." I hated when he talked with a mouthful of food. "Well then, let's go have another word with Mr. Sims," I yawned.

We headed back to across the street. "You alright, man?" Sam asked me. "Fuckin' peachy," I snapped. I threw open the the office door and stormed in. "Sims!" I shouted. "I've got some more questions for you!" He came out of the back room. "You motha fuckas better get the fuck-" I interrupted him with a left hook that made him stumble. He quickly responded with a knee to my groin, followed by three swift punches to my face. He finished his combination with a spin kick to my head that sent me flying halfway across the office.

I'm a decent brawler, but this guy hit hard and fast. Blood ran from my mouth as I stumbled to my feet. "You done fucked up now, boy," I mumbled as I rushed him. He did a side step, and swept my legs at the last second, launching me into the air. I crashed head first into a file cabinet, and slumped to the floor.

Sims had to be in his early fifties, so he was at least ten years my senior. But he was mopping the floor with me. "Watch who you callin' boy, Cracker! Now stay yo' ass down before I *really* fuck you up!" he said as Sam approached him from behind. Sims must've sensed Sam coming, because he swung a back kick up towards Sam's face, which Sam blocked. Sims turned to face his next opponent.

Sam had studied several forms of martial arts as a kid, and though he was a bit rusty, he offered much more of a challenge to Sims than I could. What ensued was a battle that rivaled many motion picture fight sequences. It lasted about five minutes, and consisted of a series of punches, kicks, and blocks that seemed so fantastic, it could've been choreographed. I stood by and watched in awe.

They were somewhat evenly matched, but Sims seemed to have a slight edge. He ended up catching Sam in an armbar, and was applying enough pressure to break the arm. Seeing Sam wince in pain made me snap out of it.

That's when I pulled the throwaway nine out of my ankle holster. I fired a shot into the ceiling to get Sims' attention. "The next one's going in your head," I warned him. "Yeah right! You fuckers are supposed to be cops." he smiled as he stood up to face me. I fired another shot, this one grazed his left arm. "Ahh! Motha fucka, you shot me!" Sims stumbled as Sam rose to his feet. He placed Sims in a choke hold that made veins protrude from his head. I casually strolled over to them and put the gun to Sims' gut.

"Now I'm gonna ask you a series of questions, and for every wrong answer you give, I'm gonna put a bullet in you. I won't kill you, but you'll beg me to, eventually. Or, you tell me what I want to know, and I'll be on my way. You'll never see me again. Understood?" Sims gasped for air.

"Ease up a little, Sam. You're choking him out. Now, I'm gonna make it easy for you, Mr. Sims. I see your wedding ring. You cooperate, and you get to go home to your wife. Otherwise, well hell... I might pay her a visit after I'm finished with you."

Sims didn't like hearing that, but it worked. He told me everything. He wasn't about to pay for his employee's stupidity, and I couldn't blame him. He had nothing to do with injuring my sister. Though he did hire the bounty hunter, it wasn't him I was after.

Jarrod O'Connor from Louisiana. After bringing in my brother in law, he left Detroit, headed for Gulfport, Mississippi. He was supposed to meet up with another bounty hunter there, and apprehend a member of a biker gang. The Wraiths. They were little known in Miami, but they were pretty infamous in the Mississippi area. The bail jumper was a guy named Cyril Gallant. Sims told us where Gallant was possibly residing. Some nightclub owned by the gang. Club Darqcyde. "Looks like we're going to Gulfport," I sighed. After leaving Sims' office, Sam and I decided it was time to get some sleep. We got a hotel a few miles away and slept for the rest of the day.

When I awoke, Sam was stuffing his face with Pizza Hut slices. "How the fuck do you stay so thin when you're constantly eating?" I yawned. "What time is it, anyway?" He glanced at his watch. "Quarter to nine." "Fuck, we gotta get going. Why didn't you wake me?" I got up and headed towards the bathroom. "You needed your beauty sleep," Sam joked. "Besides, we know where this O'Connor's gonna be at. We'll get him, man." "Damn right we will."

I shit, showered, shaved, and finished off the pizza. We left the hotel around ten o'clock. I drove most of the night. Sam took

114

over eventually. "Damn, you drive slow." I complained. "I'm doing the speed limit. Last thing we need is to get pulled over by some rookie with a hard-on for ticketing fellow officers." He was right. We were out of our jurisdiction, and we needed to fly under the radar. But I couldn't guarantee I'd do the same once we found O'Connor.

Gulfport, Mississippi. Another shithole town. Even before Katrina. But, unlike Detroit, this place had potential. Hell, with the casinos run right, this place could be as big as Atlantic City, maybe even Vegas. Perhaps that's what Gallant's gang was trying to achieve. Apparently, they owned their own casino, and were slowly taking over the area. These guys were no small time biker club. They were well organized and well connected, and taking down one of their members wouldn't be an easy task. But if we got to him before O'Connor did, we could make O'Connor come to us.

"Hey, its Fat Tuesday!" I was dozing off when Sam suddenly shouted. "What?" I was drowsy and slightly irritable. "Fat Tuesday! The last day of Mardi Gras! I haven't been there in

like ten years." he grinned. "We got a fuckin'
job to do. Fuck Mardi Gras." I frowned. "Yeah,
well fuck you." Sam mumbled. "What the fuck
did you say?" I definitely was not in the mood
for that shit. He peered over at me.

"I drop everything to drive all over this
God forsaken country for you, and I make one
observation, and you get all crazy. I know we've
got to find this asshole. But I'm just saying, I'd
like to drive over to New Orleans, its not far
from here, and take a stroll down Bourbon
street. That's all."

I didn't want to overreact, but I could-
n't help it. I guess the hours on the road was
stressing us both out. "Stop the car!" I shouted.
He hit the brakes. "You wanna go to Mardi
Gras? Go to fuckin' Mardi Gras! I'm going to
find the guy who busted up my sister's arm and
nose!" I grabbed my luggage out the trunk, and
started walking.

"Cross!" Sam shouted. "Vinny!" He
honked the horn. I kept walking. I got about
twenty feet before he sped off. 'Fuck him,' I
thought to myself, 'I don't need him anyway. I
can handle this shit myself.' I walked about a

mile before I saw a cab. I flagged it down.

I had the cabbie drop me off at a sleazy motel in Biloxi. 'Crasseux Motel'. I spent the next few hours contemplating my plan of action. I popped a few Percosets, watched some TV, and called another cab. "Destination?" The female cabbie grunted, as she scratched her mangy mullet. She was an obvious dyke. "Club Darqcyde." I smugly replied.

The ride across town was a quiet one. I observed the city, and noticed that there was a lot of destruction from a hurricane that happened a few years ago. I wondered why more wasn't being done to not only rebuild, but to fully upgrade the city. I imagined the changes I would make to the city if I was mayor. Like a taking a huge percentage of the casinos' revenues and taxing tourism like nobody's business. I always had political ambitions, but my reputation at the department wouldn't allow me to pursue those ambitions. More Vic Mackey than Sonny Crockett, I had racked up multiple complaints, and been passed up for promotion several times. I was lucky to have made Detective.

My thoughts were interrupted by a group of bikers speeding by on their choppers. "Fuckin' Mardi Gras! Wooo-hooo!" one of them was screaming. As they passed, I read the embroidery on one of their jackets. 'Wraiths'.

When I saw the club, I couldn't help but snicker. The neon sign, the raggedy looking building, the whole look of the place was low budget, compared to the clubs back home. I got out of the cab, and banged on the front door. "They don't open until midnight!" the cabbie shouted. "Yeah, give me a second."

I walked around back. I kicked the emergency exit door several times loudly. Nothing. If Gallant lived there, he was either hiding inside, or he was one of the bikers heading to Mardi Gras. I called Sam's cell phone. No answer. I was about to leave a message when I heard someone creeping up behind me.

I slowly reached for the Beretta, which was now tucked in my waist. Closer... closer...now! I spun around and pointed the gun only to see the huge eyes of the cabbie. Her hands shot up. "Please don't kill me." she whimpered. I lowered the gun. "What the fuck are you doin' sneaking up on me like that?" I demanded. "I thought you were skipping out on the fare, I'm sorry." she sobbed.

I smiled. "I'm gonna pay you, don't worry about that. But don't ever do that again, you scared the shit out of me!" "You? I just about pissed my panties!" she sighed. The thought of that made my stomach turn, so I left it at that. "I'll make it up to you right now. Take me to New Orleans." I said as I handed her a wad of cash.

The ride to New Orleans was an awkward one after what took place. We didn't speak at all. I tried reaching Sam again. No answer. Fuck him. The evening was coming to an end and nightfall was upon us. I had the cabbie drop me off near the festivities, and took a stroll.

Bourbon St. was packed, as party goers from around the country swarmed to celebrate the end of Mardi Gras. Realizing that I'd never find Gallant in the crowd, I decided to have a few drinks. I never understood what was so exciting about Mardi Gras. Alcohol, tits, beads and floats. Big Deal. Give me a handful of pills, a beer, and a strip club, and I'm right at home.

A few drinks turned into several, which turned into way too many as the night went on. I was wasted. The Percosets weren't helping either. As I stumbled out of another bar, I realized that I hadn't been this fucked up in a very long time.

I staggered into a drunken college kid wearing an ASU jacket. His beer hit the pavement. "Watch your step, dude!" He shrugged me away. "Fuck you. Dude!" I slurred as I kept walking. I shouldn't have turned my back on him, because as soon as I did, he shoved me from behind. I did a face plant in the middle of the street, as the crowd started to form a circle around me. I could hear the oohs and aahs from the onlookers, as I rose to my feet and faced the kid.

He was about 21, blonde, and appeared to be well built. Probably real popular at ASU. Probably used to being the Alpha Male, and people backing down when confronted by him. Well this wasn't ASU. I wasn't some freshman with a crush on his girlfriend. And I wasn't about to back down.

"Got a problem, old man?" He frowned, as the circle around us grew smaller. He had two friends with him, egging him on. "Get him, Todd!" they chanted. I smiled.

"Aaaaaaaah!" My battle cry sounded off as I rushed him, full speed ahead. I slammed into him, grabbing him around the waist, and taking him down. We traded a few punches on the ground, then I stood up. His chin got acquainted with my left hook, as he struggled to get back on his feet. A stiff jab to the gut made me take a step back. Once standing, he threw a wild uppercut, and missed terribly. I tagged his chin again, and followed up with a vicious right elbow to his nose. It was instantly broken, as blood rushed out of both nostrils. He was ready to fall.

He must've known he had just one shot to better his odds of winning this fight, because he took that shot. A powerful uppercut connected with my jaw. It caught me just right. Or in my case, just wrong. My legs turned into Jell-O as I tried to hang on to consciousness. Everything became blurred as I turned away from the jock.

Damn it, if only I was sober, I would've seen that punch coming. I suddenly came face to face with what appeared to be some type of mighty beast with a blue demon perched upon its back. Fading fast, I swung at the beast and hit nothing but air. Big mistake. 120,000 volts of electricity expedited my journey into unconsciousness.

"Hey, redneck! Gimme your shirt!" I opened my eyes just enough to see a very large Samoan towering over me. I looked around and realized I was in a room with about a dozen other scumbags. My head was killing me. What the fuck happened? I remembered Mardi Gras... a fight... the mounted police... I got tazed! Fuck! I was in jail.

I tried to stand, but couldn't muster the strength. I decided to continue to lay on the cold cell floor. "I said gimme your shirt, you fuckin faggot!" the topless colossus demanded. "It...won't...fit you." I mumbled. That set him off as he reached down and lifted me up by the neck. "Guess I gotta take it from you, mother fucker!" He grimaced, as he punched me twice in the stomach. "Get that cracker!" I heard someone shout as he released his grip on my neck. Once again, darkness came over me as I slumped back to the filthy floor.

My head was in unbelievable pain. That's the first thing I noticed once I regained consciousness. The awful stench was the second thing. I opened my eyes and realized I was sleeping in a puddle of my own puke. I sat up. My shirt was gone, but at least I was in a cell by myself this time.

"Hey Detective Cross, you awake I see..." The sarcastic voice belonged to a relatively small officer, sporting a boyish grin. "You gonna let me out of this cage, or what?" My whole body ached. A tall, gray haired man approached the cell. He looked haggard, and sported huge bags under his eyes. "Yes. You're getting out. But not before we have a little talk."

The old guy turned out to be the captain of the precinct. He gave me a speech about the stress he was under because of fights and other crimes committed during Mardi Gras. And how disappointed he was to see a fellow officer involved in a drunken brawl in the middle of Bourbon St.

After about 45 minutes of his lecture, he handed me a NOPD t-shirt and my belongings, and called me a cab. He did, however, keep the Beretta and the Percosets I had in my pocket. No charges filed. I thanked him for not reporting the incident to my captain, and quickly got in the cab. It was Wednesday afternoon, and I was losing time. I needed to refocus on finding O'Connor. "Where to?" the Arabic cabbie asked. "Gulfport." I muttered.

I was almost to the hotel when my cell phone rang. It was Sam. Part of me didn't even want to answer, after the bullshit I had just gone through. But I answered.

"Where the fuck have you been?" I barked. "Hey, is that how you talk to your partner?" he replied. "Especially after I've been doing some research on O'Connor, Gallant, and the whole damn Wraith gang. I've been busy, brother. And I know where Gallant is. O'Connor hasn't gotten to him yet." That news actually put a smile on my face. "Meet me at the Crasseux Motel in Biloxi in about an hour.

Room 13". I hung up. He'd find the place. It had to be the ugliest building in the city.

A knock at the door interrupted my Vicodin induced sleep. Sam arrived at the motel around eleven pm.

"Goddamn, I fuckin' dozed off. What took you so long?" I frowned. "Don't even start," he glared "You could've given me directions. Anyway, its getting late, and a fog is setting in. Lets get down to business. You look like shit, by the way."

He told me about the events that took place after we parted ways. He asked around about the Wraiths, and paid a visit to their casino. There he observed a man get tossed out of the place on his face by security. They then stripped him of his Blackjack vest.

Curious, Sam questioned the man, and found out he was just fired from the place. His name was Terrence Gilbert, and he was ready to announce all the shady business that went on in the casino. Luckily, Sam came along at the right time, and provided a listening ear.

He took Terrance to a nearby diner, and bought him a coffee. Terrence knew the layout of Iron Cross, and witnessed various well known criminals having meetings with the president of the casino. He told Sam about a back room where fugitives would hide out while preparing to leave the country. And that's where Gallant would most likely be.

Gilbert knew that following his little tell-all, he'd have to get out of town quick. But before he did, he gave Sam a security code: 1120. That code would get us access to most of the casino. But if we got caught, we'd be fucked. Security at Iron Cross was a force to be reckoned with.

"After that, I went to Bourbon Street, and had a few drinks. I tried calling you back a few times, but got your voicemail. What did you end up doing?" He asked. "Long story. Let's get to the casino," I sighed. "Excellent work, man. I appreciate you being here for me." Sam looked like he was ready to blush. "Yeah, yeah. Don't get all soft on me, Cross. Let's go get this mother fucker." Well said.

The fog was thicker than I'd seen in a long time. "You sure you can drive in this shit, man?" I nervously asked. Sam smirked. "No

sweat, it gets pretty foggy in Miami, too."
"Yeah, but not like this." I replied wearily. But
as long as *he* could see, I guess I was ok.

He started to tell me about the research
he did on the Wraiths. They started out as a
security team for Virdale Fox, a criminal mas-
termind from Baltimore. He allegedly organized
several high profile bank and armored truck
robberies back in the eighties. They never could
catch him, though. And his alibis usually consisted of 'important' people like celebrities and
other people with money.

In the nineties he went off the radar,
possibly out of the country. He moved to Biloxi
in 2002. He built a casino, and hired a bunch of
ex-cons to do security, and ex-military to train
them. He wanted to give them a 'second
chance' in life, and loyalty to him paid well.

He bought them all Harleys for
Christmas in 2004. The security team started to
grow in numbers and became infamous for the
beatings they'd give to people who tried to cheat
the casino. They called themselves Wraith Security, because they moved like ghost. You don't
see them until they want you to. But by then, it

was too late. It was shortly after Katrina, that they slowly began taking over the city. Law Enforcement couldn't touch them, hell, some of the members were cops.

While their casino was being rebuilt, they started organizing in the streets. They ran some of the small time gangs out of the area. Join, or be gone. Be gone, or be dead. They took over the meth industry, and had a hand in everything from prostitution to gun smuggling in the Gulf area. Now, simply known as The Wraiths, with over a hundred members strong, they'd become a crime syndicate. And with a well connected guy like Virdale Fox calling the shots, they were extremely dangerous.

"Sounds like we've got our work cut out for us," I sighed. "But I lost the Beretta." Sam's face wrinkled up. "You can't be serious! How the fuck did that happen?" He frowned. Feeling slightly ashamed I brushed him off. "Doesn't matter. I've still got my Sig."

He just shook his head like a disappointed parent whose underachieving child let him down once again. "So you're gonna use your personal firearm? The one you use for work?" I didn't answer him.

We had just started to cross a bridge over a small section of the Gulf of Mexico, when I saw a set of headlights that were headed in the opposite direction suddenly take a nose-dive off of the bridge. "Shit! Did you see that?" Sam yelped. "Pull over, man!" I shouted back.

He slammed the car in reverse, back onto the road, and drove up to the edge of the water. Without hesitation, I leapt out of the car, and into the freezing water. I could barely see anything as I swam deep into the gulf, chasing a shadow, and two dimming lights. Knowing what destiny awaited me at Iron Cross, I was determined to do one good deed, before unleashing my vengeful bloodlust upon who-ever stood in my way.

As I closed in on the sinking body, I saw a man struggling to live, but losing the struggle. I grabbed him, and began my ascent to the surface. I hoped no one else was in the car, but if so, they were shit out of luck. I wasn't Aquaman. I needed air too.

Once on land, Sam had a towel ready. I couldn't stop shivering, as I desperately tried to dry myself. Sam recognized the man I just saved. It was the pretty boy from the Bail Bond office in Detroit. He told us that he was on a job. "... what the fuck are you guys doing out here?" He moaned. "We're on a job too…" I replied. Sam and I started to walk back to the car.

The kid had the audacity to ask for a ride. "We're headed in the opposite direction." I grunted, as I entered the vehicle, soaking wet. Sam hopped in and hit the gas. "Fuck, what are the odds?" he chuckled.

We got to Iron Cross Casino just after midnight. It was a large casino that rested on the gulf. It resembled a 17th century battleship, and was affixed with a huge iron cross on top of it. I had already changed out of my wet clothes, and into an all black sweatsuit that Sam had in the trunk. It didn't exactly fit, I outweighed Sam by about eighty pounds. But I didn't care. It was warm and dry.

As we sat outside in the fog, I noticed a flash of lightning. "A storm is coming." Sam observed. After a long pause, I sighed. "In more ways than one, my friend. In more ways than one."

I looked at Sam, who was nervously checking the clip in his 9mm. I put my hand on his shoulder. "You know, you don't have to go through with this. You can hang out here, and I'll bring that fucker out myself." Sam looked at me like I had just eaten his dog. "Are you fuckin' kidding me? I may be a dick, but I'm not a pussy! Let's do this shit." I smiled and cocked the Sig. I tucked it in my waist and got out of the car.

We strolled through the well lit parking lot, and past the security guards at the door. I didn't make eye contact, I just kept walking. The sound of a thousand slot machines, and a multitude of voices filled my ears. People gambling happily, clueless about the casino owner's sinister activities. 'The Ace of Spades' by Motorhead was audible, but barely, over the chattering of the hundreds of late night gamblers.

We slowly paced the whole building, trying not to look suspicious. Sam pointed toward a key padded door with a sign that read 'Private'. "That's where we need to start." he said. He inconspicuously punched in the code and the door unlocked. It was just an empty room, but there was another door towards the back of it. We stepped inside, closing the door behind it, and opened the back door. It was a meeting room, big table, nice leather chairs, and a projector. I turned on the light, and tried to access a computer. Maybe I could get a more accurate layout of the building.

'Password Required'. "Fuck! This ain't gonna be easy." I groaned. "It never is." Sam replied. We exited the room, and stepped back into the main hall. "Try that room." I said, referring to a key padded door a few yards away. We moved toward the door and Sam entered the code. It opened. Inside was a long hallway with several doors on either side. "Now we're getting somewhere!" I smiled as we quickened our pace.

We took turns peeking in each room, but found only a private bar, a small movie theater, a Jacuzzi, and shit like that. "Damn, it must be nice to be a VIP here!" Sam gawked. We got to a door at the end of the hall, and I noticed a surveillance camera perched above the door. "They've probably been watching us the whole time anyway." I sighed as I opened the door.

I barely had time to react when the shots rang out. I caught one in the left shoulder, but somehow managed to barely dodge another one speeding towards my head. I tucked and rolled, and found cover behind a marble counter. "Sam- you alright?" I hollered. "Yeah!" He was still outside the room peeking in.

I pulled my Sig M2 and opened fire on the attackers. I hit one in the crotch, ruining his life forever. There were three more in the room. "You picked the wrong casino, boy!" one of them shouted, as he fired three rounds from what sounded like a 10mm. "This here is Wraith Security, and you're trespassin'!"

I fired in the direction of his voice, hitting the wall. Someone else opened fire with an AK, pinning me down. Sam silenced the assault rifle by putting three slugs in the owner's face. As the guy with the 10mm took a shot at Sam. I fired back, putting one in his head. His head snapped back from the impact if the .45

caliber bullet. Then he fell forward, on his face. The last man ran out through an open door in the back of the room. I fired twice, but missed.

"You're hit!" Sam noticed. "I'm fine." I walked over to the guy I shot in the dick. He was lying on his side, going into shock. "Cyril Gallant. Where is he?" I demanded, as I put in a new clip. "Ahhh... d-don't know... who th-that is." He whined. "Bullshit! You're a Wraith, right? Well so is he! So where is he?" "He's... n-not here."

The man was losing blood fast. His black security uniform was concealing most of it, but the puddle under him was expanding. I suddenly heard footsteps down the hall. "Incoming!" I shouted as a barrage of gunfire entered the room. I took my place behind the counter, as Sam turned over a table. The first one through the door took a round in the throat from my Sig, sending a stream of blood shooting from his esophagus.

Sam, gun in each hand, took out the next two guys with head shots, "come on, mother fuckers!" He bellowed. He slightly resembled Chow Yun Fat in some John Woo film, as he spun around and fired a few rounds at the back door, then spun back around, arms outstretched. All that was missing were the doves.

Bullets were flying in every direction, as more Wraiths entered the room. Sam's back was to the door behind him and I was trying to cover it, as well as the main door. It sounded like a shooting range, and they just kept coming. I was reloading when I heard Sam shriek in pain. I looked over to see him fall forward in slow motion. He slumped over the table, a gaping pit in the center of his back. A man with a double barreled shotgun was standing behind Sam with a devious smile on his face. My heart sank as I watched my partner take his last breath.

I rushed his killer, firing consecutive rounds at him. The first two shots hit in he gut, bending him over. The next two struck each shoulder, straightening him back up. I put one under his left cheek, and as he turned to the left, my next bullet took his nose off. I was right upon him now, and I blew out his hip with the following slug. He dropped to his knees and I put the gun to the top of his head. Liquified brains splashed up to my face, as I ended his life. For a second, I could see right through his skull to the floor after the .45 caliber slug exited his chin.

"Drop the gun!" A burly man shouted, as four more Wraiths entered the room. Without hesitation, I dove to my right. Time slowed down as the four men opened fire, the bullets barely missing me. I fired back, and as I hit the floor, I grabbed a fallen Wraith's AK. I performed a tactical roll for cover, and aimed in the general direction of the men.

Bodies went flying, as bullets tore through them, snatching the life out of them on the way out. I kept shooting until smoke filled the room, and there was no one left standing. I crawled over to Sam's shattered body, and felt a lump in my throat. "Sorry I got you into this, man." I said, trying to fight back tears.

I then realized that the mission was a failure, and I should've planned it better. Going after Gallant was a huge mistake. I should've tried to go directly for O'Connor. But I was determined to cut my losses and get out of there in one piece. I hoisted Sam onto my shoulder, and left the room, grabbing an AR15 on the way out. Anyone who got in my way was as good as dead.

I made it to the main hall when all hell broke loose. "Oh my god, he's got a gun!" an old lady screamed which sent widespread panic throughout the casino, sending patrons running for the exits. Everyone started screaming at once, like they were at a rock concert, and that hurt my concentration. Sam was getting heavy, but I just needed to make it to the exit.

I suddenly heard a .50 caliber rifle being fired from above, and the Poker table in front of me took the huge round. Poker chips and chunks of wood scattered in every direction, as the table nearly exploded. "Shiiiit!" I yelled out, and quickened my pace towards the door. I was about ten feet away, feeling like I was going to make it out, when the powerful rifle let out another shot. This one hit the intended target, and my right leg shattered as the hot slug made entry just above my calf. I might as well have been hit with a cannonball.

I could feel the bone snap, as the lower

half of my leg went flying out in front of me. I
dropped to the floor, sending Sam's corpse
flopping out in front of me. I rolled over to
face the shooter. He was on the second floor,
perched on a balcony that overlooked the main
entrance. The gun was propped up on a bipod,
and he was kneeling on the floor, exposing too
much of himself. He had a spotter next to him
who seemed to be overly excited about his
partner taking me down. He seemed more interested in congratulating the shooter, than
checking to see if I stayed down.

I aimed the AR15 at him and
unleashed 10 rounds into his body. He fell forward over the balcony, slamming on the carpet
on the first floor. The sniper took another
shot, this time striking an atm a few feet away
from me. I returned fire, and didn't stop shooting until the rifle fell from his dead hands.
Blood was pouring out of my leg, and I knew it
was going to be nearly impossible for me to
make it out alive.

More security guards emerged from the
back of the casino, firing handguns, as well as
submachine guns. I pulled myself to the oppo-

site side of the atm, using it for cover. Bullets struck slot machines, sending sparks, glass, and coins into the air. The pain of my newly amputated leg was almost unbearable, and I realized that this would be my last stand.

'Fuck it,' I thought. 'If this is how I'm gonna die, I'm taking as many of those fuckers with me as I can.' I checked the clip in the AR15. Maybe a half-dozen bullets left. Reinserting the clip, I clutched the weapon tightly, ready to make my final stand. The atm was suddenly torn apart by a barrage of bullets from a P90, and I was losing cover. Off balance, the recoil of my assault rifle nearly knocked me over as I returned fire, taking out two more Wraiths. With the gun out of ammo, I tossed it to the side and pulled out the Sig.

'This is it,' I thought, 'the final curtain.' Just then I heard someone behind me yell out "Drop your weapons, now!" I turned my head to see four police officers aiming their guns at me, along with about a dozen other cops closing in fast. I let out a premature sigh of relief when out of nowhere, one officer opened fire, setting off a chain reaction. I saw the muzzle flashes in slow motion as I attempted to roll out of harms way. I wasn't very successful, as I was struck in the left kidney and the right forearm. A pair of bullets opened up my chest, right of center. As I collapsed, my world went black.

Now as I reminisce on the whole incident, I can't help but shed a tear. Two long months have gone by since the casino shootout.

I was arrested and rushed to the hospital, where my life was spared. They couldn't do anything for my leg, and my kidney and right lung were too damaged to save. But fuck it, I'm alive.

I'm out on bond now, awaiting trial for murder. Luckily I got a judge who couldn't be bought by the Wraiths. He knew about the corruption that went on at Iron Cross, and privately told me I did Mississippi a favor by dealing a powerful blow to the Wraiths.

He promised leniency, and set my bail at $500,000, which was a good start. It was posted anonymously, and I'm currently staying at a secluded house in Jackson. I can't leave Mississippi until after the trial, if found not guilty. But I don't see that happening. I'll either get the chair, or rot in prison for the rest of my life. But I'm trying to enjoy what little freedom I've got now. Goddamn ankle bracelet. If only they put it on my prosthetic leg... Oh well.

Iron Cross Casino reopened just last week, and as I watched Virdale Fox smiling on TV, I wondered if he knew where I was staying. I didn't doubt it, due to him being so well connected. But on the other hand, I figured that if he was in fact aware of my location, I'd be dead by now.

No one at my former precinct will take calls from me, and I won't take calls from my sister. I somewhat blame her for hooking up with a convict in the first place. That's how it all started. But my thirst for revenge is the true reason I'm in my current situation. My temper ended up costing me more than I was willing to pay. My leg, my lung, my kidney, my job, my freedom, my partner. Basically, my life.

The irony is, Gallant and O'Connor were both killed the same night as the casino shootout, in a separate incident. Funny thing about life. For all the fucked up shit you do, you always end up paying for it in the end.

BULLETTIME

There's a hideous Kit-Cat clock on the wall. The one with the eyes and tail that move side to side. It freaks me out sometimes, but it's the only clock in the house. I glance at the time. It's a quarter to midnight, and I've got insomnia.

I'm watching some bullshit infomercial when I hear a knock at my door. Who the fuck can it possibly be, I wonder, as I reach for my .357 magnum. Of course I'm not allowed to have it, but fuck the rules. This is my safety we're talking about here.

"Who's there?" I shout at the door, weapon pointed. No answer. I look through the peephole, and see no one. I unlock the series of locks on the door and stick my head out. Nothing but cool night air.

Baffled, I close the door and lock it. I turn around only to have a .40 caliber HK shoved in my face. "How the fuck did you get in here?" I demand, startled. "You're back window was open. The knock at the door was just a diversion." The cold, emotionless voice is somewhat familiar, but not quite.

The lights are dim, and he's wearing a

142

hoodie. My gun is at my side, slightly behind my leg, and I'm not sure if he sees it. "So... Fox found me huh?" I ask, trying to stay calm, but my heart is racing.

"You killed a lot of people Cross. Most of them had it coming. But you fucked up. You killed a close friend of mine. And he didn't deserve to die like that. So now I'm going to end your miserable, worthless life." His voice is monotone, like some sort of cyborg from the future, programmed to terminate my existence.

"Fuckin' Wraiths," I mumble nervously. "You mother fuckers just don't quit, do you?" I'm stalling, but I'm also working up the nerve to raise my gun and attempt to take him out.

"Fuck the Wraiths," he says, annoyed. "I'm talking about Demetrios Sims." My eyebrows go up in surprise. "Who?" I'm thinking this is some joke now. Then he removes his hood. Now I remember. It's the pretty boy from the bail bonds office in Detroit. Sims' Bail Bonds.

"Remember me now, cocksucker?" He asks, and I start to get more confused. "Yeah, I remember I saved your ass from drowning. I damn sure remember *that*. But I didn't kill Sims." "Bullshit!" he roars, making me flinch. "I saw the tape." "What tape?" I ask. "Demetrios' office had a surveillance camera. I saw the fight you and your dead friend had with him. Two days later he's opening the office, and he gets gunned down. Right outside of the office, and right off camera. Explain that."

Now I'm bewildered as I don't know what he's talking about. "Fuck, I didn't kill him. I was here that night, man. You know that!" I'm not ready to die over something I didn't do.

"You drove out here after you killed him, you piece of shit. Just admit it, and I'll make this quick." He really thinks I killed his friend. Fuck it, one of us is gonna die tonight, and it damn sure ain't gonna be me.

I quickly grab his gun hand with my free hand, and raise my gun which he blocks with his free hand. We both open fire in slow motion, shooting everything but each other. I struggle for leverage, but to no avail. He's stronger than he looks.

Bullets whiz past my ear, missing by

centimeters. Two of my bullets slice through his long hair, barely missing his face, as he leans out of their path. My six shots run out quick, so I head butt him, breaking his nose. He lets out a yelp and stumbles back. He then knees me in the groin, and kicks my prosthetic leg out from under me. I lose balance, and he shoves me to the floor. I desperately look around for something else that can be used as a weapon. Nothing. "Last chance to repent your sins, Cross." my attacker snarls, as blood rushes from his nose.

Goddamn revolver. We each fired six shots, but he still has at least six left. "I didn't kill your friend." I tell him. Time doesn't slow down as I stare up at the smoking gun. Not this time. In the blink of an eye, he empties the clip into my chest. Seven rounds pass through me, splattering my heart into the floor. I feel myself go into convulsions for a few seconds. I guess it was a final fight to live. But fuck it. What for? My body stops shaking as my life comes to an end. The last thing I see is the Kit-Cat clock. Midnight.

BULLETTIME

Epilogue:

A few days after the death of Vincent Cross, the same gun that was used to kill Demetrios Sims was used in a convenience store robbery in Dearborn, Michigan. Dearborn PD caught the suspect shortly afterwards, and their crime lab linked the gun to Sims' murder. The detectives interrogated the suspect, and he broke under pressure. He admitted to the murder of Demetrios Sims.

It was a 13 year old kid. Apparently, he witnessed his drug house get shot up, and three of his cocaine dealing homies get killed. According to the kid, some "crazy Arab lookin' motha fucka" claiming that Demetrios sent him, robbed them of two kilos of cocaine and some cash. The kid tried to take the assailant out, but his gun jammed, and he was beaten unconscious.

The kid blamed Sims for the killings. The place he called home was gone, and so were the only 'family' he had. So he did what he felt he had to do, he took revenge, and killed Sims outside of his office.

Funny thing is, shortly after his arrest, the kid was bailed out of jail anonymously by the same company that bailed out Vincent Cross just a few weeks earlier. Looks like Sims' Bail Bonds is still in business. Unofficially, of course.

And make no mistake about it, when the so-called "crazy Arab lookin' motha fucka", known to us as Ash Calibre catches up to him, that kid is going to have hell to pay.

E. FAISON

BULLETTIME

Thank you for reading BulletTime.

Be on the look out for future titles from E. Faison.

Coming soon:

January 2009: untitled Ash Calibre book

Summer 2010: BulletTime vol.2

TBD 2011: Serial Killer Diaries

TBD: Bloodlust in the Valley of the Sun

E. FAISON

BULLETTIME